W9-CLZ-740

TO

FRANKIE MCLOUGHLIN

PATRIOT, STUDENT, ATHLETE

HE GAVE ALL HE HAD FOR HIS COUNTRY AND HIS TEAM

Frankie McLoughlin was the Long Island University mascot when he was six years old. After graduating high school, he played with the LIU freshman team, and when World War II was declared, volunteered for service. He was killed in an airplane crash in the Pacific area.

COACH CLAIR BEE, 1948

TO THE MEMORY OF

COACH CLAIR FRANCIS BEE

(1896–1983)

HUSBAND, FATHER, EDUCATOR, COACH, MENTOR, AND AUTHOR

He believed in and dedicated his life and efforts to *you*, the youth of the world. He was blessed with the precious gift of recognizing and developing the best in everyone.

RANDY, CINDY, AND MICHAEL CLAIR FARLEY, 1998

BOOKS BY CLAIR BEE

TECHNICAL
Basketball
Winning Basketball Plays
The Basketball Coach's Handbook
The Clair Bee Basketball Quiz Book
Basketball for Future All-American Stars
Basketball for Everyone
Make the Team in Basketball

THE CLAIR BEE BASKETBALL LIBRARY
The Science of Coaching
*Basketball Fundamentals and Techniques: Individual
    and Team Basketball Drills*
Man-to-Man Defense and Attack
Zone Defense and Attack

FICTION
The Chip Hilton Stories
Touchdown Pass
Championship Ball
Strike Three
Clutch Hitter
A Pass and a Prayer
Hoop Crazy
Pitchers' Duel
Dugout Jinx
Freshman Quarterback
Backboard Fever
Fence Busters
Ten Seconds to Play

Fourth Down Showdown
Tournament Crisis
Hardcourt Upset
Pay-Off Pitch
No-Hitter
Triple-Threat Trouble
Backcourt Ace
Buzzer Basket
Comeback Cagers
Home-Run Feud
Hungry Hurler
Fiery Fullback

11/23

Chip Hilton Sports Series

#1

Touchdown Pass

Coach Clair Bee

Foreword by Bobby Knight

**BROADMAN
&HOLMAN
PUBLISHERS**

Nashville, Tennessee

© 1998 by Randall and Cynthia Bee Farley
All rights reserved. Printed in the United States of America

0-8054-1686-2

Published by Broadman & Holman Publishers,
Nashville, Tennessee
Senior Acquisitions & Development Editor:
William D. Watkins
Page Design: Anderson Thomas Design, Nashville, Tennessee
Typesetting: PerfecType, Nashville, Tennessee

Subject Heading: FOOTBALL—FICTION / YOUTH
Library of Congress Card Catalog Number: 98-28092

Library of Congress Cataloging-in-Publication Data
Bee, Clair.
    Touchdown pass / Clair Bee ; edited by Cynthia Bee
Farley and Randall K. Farley.
        p.   cm. — (Chip Hilton sports series ; v. 1)
    Updated ed. of a work published in 1948.
    Summary: In the process of learning to go beyond
himself and to reach out to others, high school star football player Chip Hilton uncovers an act of sabotage at the
local pottery.
    ISBN 0-8054-1686-2 (alk. paper)
    [1. Football—Fiction. 2. Sportsmanship—Fiction.]
I. Farley, Cynthia Bee, 1952– . II. Farley, Randall K.,
1952– . III. Title. IV. Series: Bee, Clair. Chip Hilton
sports series ; v. 1.

PZ7.B38196To   1998
[Fic]—dc21   98-28092
                                                    CIP
                                                     AC

1 2 3 4 5 02 01 00 99 98

Contents

CONTENTS

Foreword

THERE IS nothing that could be a greater honor for me than to be able to write the foreword to the new editions of the Chip Hilton books written by Clair Bee and revised by his daughter Cindy and son-in-law Randy.

I can remember that in the early and midfifties when I was in junior high and high school, there was nothing more exciting, outside of actually playing a game, than reading one of the books from Coach Bee's Chip Hilton series. He wrote twenty-three books in all, and I bought and read each one of them during my student days. His books were about the three sports that I played—football, basketball, and baseball—and had the kind of characters in them that every young boy wanted to imagine that he was or could become.

Chip Hilton himself was a combination of everything that was good, right, and fair in athletic competition. His accomplishments on the field, on the floor, or on the diamond were the things that made every boy's dreams. Henry Rockwell was the kind of coach that every boy wanted to play for, and he knew how to get the best out of every boy who played for him.

My mother and grandmother used to take me shopping with them in Akron and would leave me at the bookstore in O'Neil's department store with $1.25 to purchase the Chip Hilton book of my choice. It would invariably take me at least two hours to decide which of these wonderfully vivid episodes in athletic competition, struggle, and accomplishment I would purchase.

As I read my way through the entire series, I learned there was a much greater value to what Clair Bee had written than just the lifelike portrayal of athletic competition. His books had a tremendous sense of right and wrong, what was fair and what wasn't, and what the word *sportsmanship* was all about.

During the first year I was at the United States Military Academy at West Point as an assistant basketball coach, I had the opportunity to meet Clair Bee, the author of those great stories that were such an integral part of my boyhood dreams. After all, no boy could have ever read those wonderful stories without imagining himself as Chip Hilton.

Clair Bee became one of the two most influential people in my career as a college coach. I have never met a man whose intelligence I have admired more. No one person has ever contributed more to the game of basketball in the development of the fundamental skills, tactics, and strategies of the game than Clair Bee during his fifty years as a teacher of the sport. I strongly believe that the same can be said of his authorship of the Chip Hilton series.

FOREWORD

It seems that every day I am asked by a parent, "What can be done to interest my son in sports?" Or "What is the best thing I can do for my son, who really has shown an interest in sports?" For the past thirty-three years, when I have been asked those questions, I have always answered by saying, "Have your son read about Chip Hilton." Then I've explained a little bit about the Chip Hilton series.

The enjoyment that a young athlete can get from reading the Chip Hilton series is just as great today as it was for me more than forty years ago. The lessons that Clair Bee teaches through Chip Hilton and his exploits are the most meaningful and priceless examples of what is right and fair about life that I have ever read. I have the entire series in a glass case in my library at home. I still spend a lot of hours browsing through those twenty-three books.

As a coach, I will always be indebted to Clair Bee for the many hours he spent helping me learn about the game of basketball. As a person, I owe an even greater debt to him for providing me with the most memorable reading of my youth through his series on Chip Hilton.

BOB KNIGHT

Head Basketball Coach, Indiana University

CHAPTER 1

The "Rock"

WILLIAM "CHIP" HILTON felt as though all the scrubs and half the varsity had used him as the tackling dummy. He could scarcely breathe, but in spite of lying at the bottom of a sweaty heap of tangled arms and legs, he felt a glow of satisfaction. The football was safely cradled against his ribs.

One of Chip's long legs was drawn up until it nearly touched his chin strap and, under this protective space, the ball was wrapped up in both arms, fiercely gripped by long fingers.

The "Rock" had said to protect the ball at all costs. Well, he'd protected the ball all right—at the cost of several knees and elbows jammed in his face.

The athlete sprawled on Chip's head took a long time to get up. Chip spat out a mouthful of grit and dirt. He'd been roughed up a little too much on that play.

"All right, get up! Let's have a little life," Coach Rockwell growled through clenched teeth. "What an offense! Two yards in three downs! Collins, take Taylor's place at quarterback. Someone on this squad ought to be able to do a little blocking!"

Cody Collins was rough and rugged. He hurried toward the varsity as Jordan "Air" Taylor walked dejectedly over to join the scrubs.

Back in the huddle, a tired Chip Hilton draped his long arms thankfully across the strong shoulders of Ted Williams and Speed Morris and let his glance wander beyond the ball and along the defensive line. For just a second his gray eyes narrowed on Joel "Fats" Ohlsen at left tackle, and then he shifted his glance to meet Chris Badger's challenging, defiant glare. Unwaveringly, their eyes met and held. An unspoken challenge passed between them.

A vicious jab in the stomach jarred Chip back to the football business at hand. Cody Collins, crouching in the middle of the huddle, snapped, "Come on, Hilton. Stop daydreaming! Heads up, gang. Hilton on a straight buck over right guard. Ball on—"

Chip's temper flared. "Next time you punch me, Collins, I'll—"

"What's going on here?" bellowed an angry Coach Rockwell pushing his way into the huddle. "Now, I want no more arguing. Quarterback calls the plays and everyone else keeps quiet. Understand? All right, Collins, let's have a play."

Collins dropped down on one knee inside the huddle, eyeing Hilton with unveiled hate. "Hilton on a straight buck over right guard," he said. "Ball on the count of four. Let's do it!"

THE "ROCK"

They broke out of the huddle in a rhythmic half-trot and took their places in the double wingback formation—Chip in the fullback slot, four and a half yards back of center; Collins at quarterback; Ted Williams and Speed Morris on the wings.

The line was unbalanced to the right, and Chip involuntarily shifted his eyes toward the hole between the two guards, Eric "Red" Schwartz and Robby Leonard. "There I go," he muttered to himself, "tipping 'em off again."

"1-2-3-4."

The spiral snap from Nick Trullo was high and to his left. It slowed him somewhat and brought him upright a bit. At that, he was right on Collins's heels as they hit the line. But it was no good—there wasn't a sign of a hole—only an avalanche of defensive players who had swarmed to the point of attack. Chip had no alternative.

He left his feet in a headlong dive, parallel to the ground. As he went over the top, the whole line seemed to rise up as a wave and hurl him backward. He landed facedown on the turf just as Coach Rockwell's whistle killed the play. But it wasn't the end for Chip. He barely had time to duck before Fats Ohlsen's 220 pounds landed directly on his head.

When Chip managed to stand and join the huddle, it seemed composed of twenty dim and hazy figures instead of ten. Chip tried to count helmets, but it was impossible—they just wouldn't hold still.

"Hilton over right guard on the count of two."

The ball floated back to him like a balloon. Everything seemed to be moving in slow motion as he reached for the ball and again drove to the right of center. His head was up, all right, and he was looking for a hole, but again there just wasn't any. It seemed as if the whole defensive team met him at the line of scrimmage and piled on. The ball flew out of his numb fingers.

Chip's head was buzzing. Dazed, he struggled to his feet and, from a great distance, heard Coach Rockwell bellowing, "That's enough of that! I can't look at that kind of football any longer. Everyone hit the bleachers!"

Chip was still groggy, but a fierce resentment toward the unfairness of the afternoon's practice was beginning to grow in his mind. Time and again Coach Rockwell had criticized his slow starting and his inability to gain through the line. Line? What line? There wasn't any line other than Biggie Cohen.

He dropped down on the first row of the bleachers, his wide shoulders slumped forward, weary under the weight of his sweat-soaked uniform. He was dead tired, almost too tired to lift his head. His gray eyes were half-closed, and he kneaded a bruised leg with long fingers as he fought desperately to keep alert. Sharp anger over the dirty tactics used against him all afternoon smoldered bitterly in his thoughts. A player could take just so much.

Although it was already the second week of September, no wind stirred across the practice field to relieve the rays of the hot sun. Perspiration poured from under Chip's short-cropped blond hair, running in little streams over his face, but he made no move to mop it away.

Coach Henry "Rock" Rockwell, Valley Falls's veteran football mentor, may have been tired, too, but he didn't act as if he were. His black eyes snapped viciously, and he bit off his words as he paced in front of the weary players who were gratefully relaxing on the bleachers. From time to time, he stopped and kicked at a clump of grass, his whole being registering disgust.

THE "ROCK"

"I thought you fellows were going to report in shape! Humph! In shape! We've been practicing nearly two weeks, and there isn't a man on this squad who can run a hundred yards without falling on his face. This isn't a football team—it's a bunch of wimpy couch potatoes! I want athletes!"

He shifted the football he was holding from one tanned hand to the other as he looked along the row of players, scrutinizing each player's face.

"Football is over by Thanksgiving! At the rate you're going, you'll probably get in condition just in time to run a race with Santa Claus! Some of you act as if you have made the team; just because the turnout is light, you think all you've got to do is put on a uniform and show up. Well, you've got a big surprise coming."

Coach Rockwell's sharp eyes darted from one player to the next as he spoke. It was clear he was concerned about the squad. He was also worried about the coming season. Only four regulars remained from the previous year's squad: Hilton, left end; Cohen, left tackle; Morris, hard-running halfback; and Williams, a guard.

The coaching staff's worries didn't end there. The other candidates, last year's reserves and the usual newcomers, were much too light and inexperienced to handle Valley Falls's powerful double wingback attack.

Last night at home and again that afternoon before practice, Coach Rockwell and his two assistants, Bill Thomas and Chet Stewart, had tried to figure out some sort of lineup capable of using the bruising offense that had made the Big Reds the intimidators of the league. But it just wasn't happening. In desperation, he had nearly sold himself on the idea of a change. He would have to do something soon; the opening game of the season was only two weeks away. For the past fifteen days he had been driving the squad unmercifully, hoping to compensate for the players' lack of experience and smaller numbers by getting them into prime playing condition. At the same time, he had been analyzing each player, trying to determine where each might fit into the still undecided offense.

"Football's a fast man's game—not a lazy man's game! If you don't want to play badly enough to get in shape, just remember to bring a nice, soft cushion to the games. Then you and I can sit on the bench and watch real athletes play who love this game enough to get in shape."

Chip raised his head and rubbed the back of his neck. Fats Ohlsen had really popped him on that last hit. Well, he wouldn't be caught again. If that was the way Ohlsen wanted it, OK. The movement attracted Coach Rockwell's attention, and he stopped directly in front of Hilton, his black eyes boring steadily into those of the startled player.

"Fullback, huh? Chip Hilton, the Sugar Bowl's official football wannabe, wanted to be a backfield star, but he didn't have the time to do a little running in the summer. No sir! Hah! I've been watching you try to imitate a fullback all afternoon. Drive? Why, you couldn't break out of a wet—"

Someone snickered, and Coach Rockwell whipped his head around and pointed a finger in the direction of a short, heavyset boy seated in the second row. "That goes for you, too, Badger!"

Christopher Badger, open-mouthed, shook his head in mock innocence but said nothing. He had been a reserve guard the year before, but Coach Rockwell had moved him over with the backfield candidates at the first practice. Last year's fullback, Tim Murphy, had graduated, and Coach Rockwell was trying to decide whether Badger or Hilton could better fill the slot.

Hilton and Badger presented extremes in fullback types. Chris was stocky, with short, heavy legs that churned with precision and power when he drove into a line. His experience in pulling out of a guard position to run interference had given him training in the use of quick, digging steps that got his 180 pounds exploding on the snap.

Chip Hilton was tall, all arms and legs. Not as quick a starter as Badger, he made up for that deficiency once he was under way, with long, effortless strides that gobbled up unbelievable yardage. His change of pace and deceptive speed had enabled him to outmaneuver practically every opposing back who'd been assigned to stop his pass-snaring the previous year.

Rockwell hadn't stopped with those moves. He had shifted Ted Williams from regular left guard to right halfback. It was clear to everyone Coach Rockwell had planned to build his attack around his only backfield holdover, Speed Morris, and was trying to surround him with good blockers. Morris could start fast and "turn on a dime and give you change." Although last year had been his first as a regular, he had been a unanimous All-State selection.

"Cody, come here."

Coach Rockwell's eyes drilled into those of the stocky little quarterback as Collins left Badger's side.

"Now, show me how to use a cross-body block on an end. Yes, block *me!* Come out here and take your position and take me out—for keeps!"

Cody assumed his quarterback position and began his snap count: "36-19-48-27."

TOUCHDOWN PASS

Pivoting on his right foot, he drove out toward Coach Rockwell, body low, head up, and arms swinging. He faked to the right with his head and then swung shoulders and upper body to the left, striking the coach just above the knees with his right side and thigh. All the time, his feet were digging in short, quick strides. Rockwell was forced back and kept his feet only with difficulty.

"Good! That's the way to hit!" Rock declared. "Let's see the rest of you block like that! Now, I want all of you backs to start lifting your knees high." Rockwell brought his right knee up to his chin. "Like this, see? Bring your knees up to your chin every time you hit the line. Understand? I want you ball carriers to tuck the ball up under your outside arm—away from the tackler—and keep that other arm and hand out there for a straight-arm.

"Protect that ball all the time. Don't forget, opposing linemen are taught to *tackle the ball,* to steal or take it away from you. They tackle the ball every time they get a chance, and they get a chance every time you hit the line! Don't risk a fumble! When you're hit, wrap that ball up tight with both arms.

"I want to see some semblance of straight-arming; get your forearm up close to your chest, like this—get it? Then use the heel of your hand to knock tacklers out of the way. Understand?

"Keep your head up when you hit the line too. A good back keeps his head up and his eyes open, and when he sees daylight, he *explodes* out beyond the scrimmage line. Come down here, Speed!"

Speed Morris leaped from the bleachers and landed lightly next to the coach. He and Rockwell looked like two of a kind—both were strongly built, with powerful legs and broad shoulders.

"Here, take the ball and show us how to hold it. That's right. Notice the spread of Speed's fingers over the end of the ball. Now show us how to wrap the ball up when you're tackled."

Speed's powerful black hand slid the ball around in front of his body, and, bending over, he placed his free hand on the end of the ball, which previously had been held under the armpit. The ball could hardly be seen.

"Good! Thanks, Morris. Now, when you backs cut off-tackle, or outside the end, I want speed! If the blockers don't get out of your way, *run up their backs!* Time your running; know *when* to cut back, *when* to outrun a tackler, *when* to use a change of pace."

Chip was wide awake now. Coach really knows his football. Guess he was right, too, about being in shape. Still, he could have left out that stuff about the Sugar Bowl. Rock seemed to forget he *had* to work there. If it wasn't for his job at the Sugar Bowl, things would be tougher at home.

Chip remembered Rock's letter to all the varsity candidates that summer, urging them to report in condition. Rockwell was always on top of things, always thinking ahead. Well, he'd better be thinking ahead himself if he wanted to make good as a back. Maybe he should have held on to his position at end. He knew *that* one. On the offense, he could box a tackle or catch passes with the best of them. On the defense, no team had turned his and Biggie Cohen's side of the line last year. Still, he'd always wanted to be a back. He could run and pass and kick. Maybe there was some other backfield quality he lacked. Maybe Badger *would* make a better fullback.

He focused his eyes on the two players who were seated on each side of Chris Badger. Cody Collins was gunning for the quarterback job, and Fats Ohlsen was trying to earn a spot at tackle. Both were good prospects, and both had made it clear they were determined to keep Chip Hilton from making the fullback position. The afternoon scrimmage had proved that.

Badger and Collins had been buddies for years. *A whole lot like Speed and me,* Chip was thinking. It was natural that Cody should pull for Chris to snag the fullback job, but he couldn't understand their sudden friendship with Ohlsen.

Joel Ohlsen rubbed most people the wrong way on sight. The only son of one of the town's wealthier families, Joel enjoyed showing off his money and putting other people down. Joel's mean temperament and arrogance had already antagonized almost all the athletes. Ohlsen and Hilton's adversarial relationship went way back to elementary school days when Joel had continually tormented and bullied Chip. The third-grade fight hadn't lasted long. Chip had fought like a veritable wildcat, and his damaged ego drove him to defend his pride despite Joel's size.

Someone had stopped that first fight, but it hadn't ended there. Joel had instigated other verbal and physical exchanges throughout middle school, and the animosity lingered. He still liked to yank Chip's chain. Chip dismissed the thoughts. Right now football was the thing. He concentrated on Coach Rockwell's words.

"That's enough about condition. Get in shape or sit the bench! It's up to you. Twice around the field and hit the showers!"

Three tired and dispirited coaches sat in the bleachers, watching the squad circle the field. Rockwell's eyes

THE "ROCK"

followed Hilton and Morris, jogging side by side, matching stride for stride on the far side of the field. Chip and Speed had been friends since elementary school, when the Morris family arrived in Valley Falls so Speed's dad could set up his new legal practice.

The Rock watched in silence as the two best friends completed their first lap and made the fourth and final turn on the track toward the stadium gate and the finish line. Suddenly, as if unleashed by a starter's gun, the two boys flashed forward. Speed's quick, digging strides propelled him immediately into the lead. The advantage lasted only a few yards, however, for Hilton's long strides gradually ate up the distance between the two flying figures, and at the finish he forged a step ahead.

"Hilton's long legs can move," said Thomas dryly.

"They sure can," confirmed Stewart. "Kinda piled it on him today, didn't you, Coach?" he ventured.

"Speakin' of pilin' it on," drawled Thomas, "seems like Ohlsen plays his best football *after* the whistle."

"You're right, Bill," Rockwell nodded his head reflectively. "I should have done something about that. Piling-on is dirty football, and I won't stand for it. Just had my mind too busy with other things, right then." He paused. "I'm a little sorry I said that about the Sugar Bowl too. Hilton *does* have a pretty rough road. School and football are enough to keep most boys busy, to say nothing of working after school."

"There's more to that little feud between Hilton and Ohlsen than dirty football, Rock," said Stewart. "That quarrel started in grade school."

"Look, Chet, there's no time out here for feuds or fights. I never could see teammates fighting, and I don't aim to start. Right now, my interest in Chip Hilton is to determine whether he has what it takes to play fullback. It's either Hilton or Badger for the job."

"I like Badger," said Thomas softly. "He hits harder and starts faster."

"You *would!*" Stewart laughed. "But Badger's a guard. Once a guard, always a guard. I'll take Hilton! He can run, pass, and kick. What else does he need?"

"Just a little bit of experience behind the line, maybe," said Rockwell. "Looks a lot like his dad did, all those years back, when he first came out for the team. I can still see him—tall, skinny, and energetic. Big Chip could *really* run."

"All-American at State, wasn't he?" asked Thomas.

"Sure! Two years!" Coach Rockwell reflected. "All-State and All-American in football and basketball and good enough for major league baseball if he'd wanted to play. But, chemistry came first with him, that is, after Mary Carson. He'd always wanted to be a chief chemist here at the pottery, and chief chemist he was!"

"We'd better get our offense started pretty soon," ventured Stewart.

They sat in silence. Coach Rockwell, submerged in thought, was looking past the scoreboard emblazoned with a red and white VF at the end of the field. Suddenly, he sprang to his feet. His voice was sharp and his black eyes were snapping. "My mind's made up! We're going to use the T-formation. It worked with a similar team here at Valley Falls years ago. But, we'll add a few new twists to one of the oldest formations in the game. With a light, fast squad, it's our key to success!"

CHAPTER 2

The Hilton A. C.

SPEED MORRIS slammed on the brakes and slid his beloved Mustang to a stop in front of the Hilton home as Chip leaped to the sidewalk with a perfect basketball one-two smack of his feet. Three long strides and a leap, and Chip cleared the wooden gate. Landing on the balls of his feet, he turned to wave, but Speed and his car had already rounded the corner.

"Two of a kind," Chip muttered. "No matter where they're going—the two of them—they're always in a hurry!"

Coach Rockwell had poured it on him today. Yet, he felt a little better after the workout. So far, the Rock was giving him first call on the fullback job. Whether he could hold it or not was up to him. Passing through the hallway he glanced at the big couch in the living room. For a moment he was tempted to relax, but, tired as he was, he couldn't resist the stronger call of the "Hilton Athletic Club."

TOUCHDOWN PASS

The Hilton A. C. was the big backyard of the Hilton home where Chip's father, long before his death, had erected a set of goal posts, a pair of baskets, and a pitcher's mound and home plate.

Chip stopped on the back porch. Several baseball bats were leaning in a corner. He carefully selected one and stood there weighing it in his hands. Then he assumed a left-handed batting stance and leveled the bat through in a full swing. After a few minutes, he grunted in satisfaction, picked up an old, battered basketball, and headed to the court.

As he dribbled the ball toward the basket, he glanced at the mound and the home plate his father had built. There wasn't a day that went by when Chip didn't think about his father. Until the accident several years before, William "Big Chip" Hilton had tried to develop Chip into a pitcher. Although he had the build for the position, few people noticed his long arms and wide, sloping shoulders. His friendly face, gray eyes, and wide smile were as far as most people got. Chip Hilton was a lean, long-limbed, overgrown teenager who had not yet filled out but who showed promise of tremendous power.

Directly against the rear fence were the goal posts. Chip remembered his father's friends had laughed at them, except Mr. Andrews, who had been such a great friend of the Hiltons. Evening after evening, Mr. Andrews would lean over the back fence beaming his interest. But he was gone too. The Andrewses had moved away several months ago, and last week a moving van had brought new neighbors. Mrs. Hilton had said a tall boy about Chip's age and a younger girl were in the family.

Big Chip Hilton's patient foresight in erecting the goal posts had helped develop his son into a fine kicker.

THE HILTON A. C.

Chip's long legs were filled with smooth-flowing, coordinated power that could send a football booming a consistent fifty yards.

Whenever he was alone, Chip practiced basketball, playing a little mental game with himself, counting hits and misses. Now, as he shot from different spots around the court, some of Coach Rockwell's sports slogans ran through his mind. One, in particular, was a favorite: "You learn to swim in the winter and skate in the summer."

Guess that must have been a part of Dad's philosophy, too, he reflected. *Dad made me kick footballs and shoot baskets in the summer.* Then in the winter, he'd always talk baseball and football even though everyone else was concerned with basketball.

As he scooped up the ball and drove on an imaginary defender, Chip was suddenly conscious he was being watched. He turned toward the fence, half expecting to see Mr. Andrews. Instead, he was surprised to face a tall boy wearing round-rimmed glasses and a younger, pony-tailed girl watching him intently.

It was a veritable giant who had been so engrossed in Chip's practice. The boy was several inches taller than Chip and well-proportioned. Chip recovered from his surprise and smiled a hello, which was warmly returned. The two boys stood measuring each other for a brief second.

"Are you two just gonna keep staring at each other?" giggled the girl.

Chip laughed. "My name is Hilton, Bill Hilton. Everybody calls me Chip, though."

"Mine's Jacob Browning," the big boy smiled shyly. "This little dweeb here is my sister, Ashley Suzanne, and we're—"

TOUCHDOWN PASS

"My *name* is Suzy, Jacob George Browning, and I'm *not* a dweeb. I'm almost in high school. Besides, you're a dork!"

Chip, amused by their performance, returned a smile. "Guess we're neighbors. C'mon over and let's shoot a few. Say, how tall are you, anyway?"

"I'm six feet seven inches without my shoes on."

"Ever play basketball?"

"Sure, it's a great game, but I'm not very good. I'm not much of an athlete."

"That's an understatement," quipped Suzy.

Jacob turned and asked pointedly, "Isn't it time for you to go running? I think I heard Mom call you."

"Well, athlete or no athlete, you're one thing, for sure! Know what it is?"

"Klutzy is about all I can think of," Jacob responded, glaring his sister into silence.

"Nope! You're one of about ten thousand! There are only about ten thousand men and boys in the United States who are six feet seven or over in height. That's something!"

The three were soon at ease with one another, and Chip learned much about his new neighbors. Jacob Browning was a sophomore in high school and, although he had gone out for his former high school basketball team, he had not been able to make the squad. He loved basketball but was sure he would never be able to play well. School work, however, came easily for him.

Chip discovered Suzy, a gifted eighth-grader, loved running and tormenting her older brother.

Their father had lost his job in Gainesville, Indiana, and they had moved to Valley Falls, hoping Mr. Browning could get a position in the pottery.

THE HILTON A. C.

Chip measured Browning's big body. "Play football?"

"I don't much like football. I'd like to try basketball again this year though. But if Dad doesn't get a job soon, I guess I won't have the chance 'cause we'll probably move again."

Mary Hilton strode confidently through the telephone company parking lot, as the autumn breeze swept through her shoulder-length blond hair. She was looking forward to getting home. Her job as a supervisor was demanding, but she enjoyed the responsibilities and the camaraderie of her coworkers. Years earlier, having earned an associate's degree, she had joined the company in an entry-level position while Bill Hilton was still in college.

The Hilton home at 131 Beech Street was a short drive from the phone company. She always enjoyed arriving home by 5:30 so she and Chip could have dinner together before he went to his job at the Sugar Bowl. It was the high point of her day. Neither she nor Chip would have felt right if they didn't share their dinner hour together every evening.

Mail in hand—the meowing cat trailing after her—Mary entered the kitchen. She knew where she'd find Chip. He spent every possible minute in the backyard.

With both hands on the sill of the kitchen window, she watched Chip and the tall boy and younger girl from next door, talking and laughing under the basket. She never could get over the marked resemblance Chip bore to his father. Her thoughts went back to happier days and evenings like this . . . when, after dinner, Chip's father would evade her knowing, gray eyes and start for the backyard with his old catcher's glove.

TOUCHDOWN PASS

Mary Hilton had always teased Big Chip, calling him a "has-been," but deep inside she was enormously proud of him. She had never gotten over her admiration of Big Chip's commitment to achieving his educational goals while becoming an All-American at State. Bill's high school sweetheart, she had attended business school, and after his graduation from the university, the young couple had married and made their home in Valley Falls. The Hilton home was blessed with happiness and love.

Big Chip had spent many years in the pottery, working his way up until he became the chief chemist. Between times, he had prepped Little Chip for athletic success. But, after all his patient work, he did not live to see his son play on a high school team. The year before Little Chip entered Valley Falls High School, swift, heartbreaking disaster struck. Big Chip was crushed under a pile of falling saggers in the kiln. A kilnsman was piling saggers of delicate ceramic ware, one on top of the other, and had not noticed the protective casing on the bottom was cracked. Just as Big Chip entered the kiln, the layers started to topple. Without a second's hesitation, Big Chip threw himself headlong against the kilnsman's body, knocking him clear. Big Chip had nearly made it too.

Although J. P. Ohlsen, the renowned owner of the pottery, rushed three specialists to Hilton's bedside, their efforts simply weren't enough. Big Chip fought all the way, but the odds were too great: his chest had been crushed.

William Hilton Sr. had been tough with Little Chip, but he was proud of him too. He had always laughed with such pleasure when he and his son were referred to as Big Chip and Little Chip. Somewhere along the line after his father's death, Chip lost the first part of his nickname. Mary Hilton couldn't remember exactly when it happened, but suddenly he was no longer Bill, Billy, or Little Chip—but simply, Chip.

Her reverie was broken as Chip bounded the back porch steps three at a time, rushing to give his mother a hug, "Hi ya, Mom."

"Hello, honey! You look tired. Hard workout today?"

"Sure was, Mom. Guess what? Get this, Coach started me at the fullback spot today on the first team!"

"He did? Well," she added, laughing, "why not? Like it?"

"Yeah! Don't know whether or not I can handle it, though. Don't know whether I'm fast enough."

"You can't learn everything there is to know about a new position in a day, sweetie. Maybe you just need more practice. I see you met two of our new neighbors."

"You mean Jacob. Jacob Browning and his sister, Suzy. You know how tall he is? Six feet seven!"

"He looks *seven* feet seven to me," Mary laughed. "He sure ought to make a good basketball center!"

"You got that right! That's all we need to have a championship team this year, Mom. If we had a big center like that, I could play forward, maybe."

"I thought this was the football season," she teased, smiling.

"It is, Mom. But, if Jacob's dad is—" He stopped in the middle of the sentence, reflecting. "Jacob . . . Jake . . . that's not gonna work. He needs a cool basketball nickname. He's tall. Stretch, Tip, Topper, Taps. That's it! I'll call him Taps!" he declared.

"You know, Mom, Jacob—er, Taps is awfully worried about his father. Lost his job for some reason. He's a pottery man too! He's been in the pottery business all his life. Just moved here from Indiana. They moved to Valley Falls because he thinks he's got a shot at getting a job here in the pottery. Taps said otherwise they might move again. They just got here, so why would they move? I'm going to ask Mr. Schroeder about a job for him."

"Good idea. But right now, we better get busy on dinner, or you'll be late," quipped Mary Hilton as she playfully tossed Chip a head of lettuce to wash.

Petey Jackson, the Sugar Bowl's popular manager and self-proclaimed sports guru, looked up as Chip entered the store. His sharp eyes twinkled mischievously.

"Hi ya, fullback!" he greeted.

"Who told you?"

"Speed. Just left!"

"Comin' back?"

"Yeah. Said he'd be back later."

"I've got to see the boss. Where is he?"

"Storeroom. G'wan back."

John Schroeder, owner of Valley Falls Pharmacy and the adjoining Sugar Bowl, looked up as Chip opened the door. "Hello, Chip," he greeted, "how's football these days?"

"Fine! Mr. Schroeder, could . . . could we use another employee here in the store?"

The lanky, friendly-faced man, who had been more like a father to Chip than an employer, regarded the tall, blond-headed boy questioningly.

"I don't know, Chip," he responded. "We've got about all the help we need right now. *You* don't need help, do you?"

"No, I—I guess not—but a new guy just moved next door to us, Mr. Schroeder. His father's out of work and I thought maybe—Well, I thought maybe you might give him a job doing something. He's all right, Mr. Schroeder, and besides he's six feet seven and likes basketball."

"Oh, so that's it!" John Schroeder smiled. Then he studied Chip's worried, gray eyes.

"What does his father do, Chip?"

"He's a pottery man."

"Did he try to get a job at the pottery?"

"I don't know—he—I don't know. Jacob—that's the boy—said his father knew about an opening and sent his résumé but didn't know anyone and was awfully discouraged."

"If he's a pottery man, Chip, maybe I can help him. I'll ask J. P. Ohlsen to give him a chance."

"Would you, Mr. Schroeder? You really wouldn't mind asking Mr. Ohlsen to give him a job?"

"Certainly, I'll ask! Why not? Is he a good family man, Chip? Sober? Hard-working?"

"I'm sure he is, Mr. Schroeder. His son and daughter are very nice. I get the feeling he just has to have this job!"

"Don't worry about it, Chip. I'll ask J. P. about it over lunch tomorrow. First thing you know, he'll probably be working at the pottery."

CHAPTER 3

Poor Sportsmanship

SOAPY SMITH, standing in front of the bulletin board, read the program for the afternoon's practice. His freckled face contorted in a grimace of pain. "Oh, no!" he groaned. "Look at that schedule! Four o'clock, grass drill; 4:15, group work. That Thomas'll kill me yet; 4:45, sprints. Five o'clock, dummy scrimmage; 5:30, tackling dummy; 5:45, live tackling. Six o'clock, scrimmage and dress rehearsal. Who's bein' funny around here with that 'dress rehearsal' stuff?"

"Yeah," someone said, "and what time does Old Gibraltar think we have dinner at our house?"

Clarence "Pop" Brown, Valley Falls's veteran trainer, wrapped the last bit of tape on Biggie Cohen's ankle and straightened up. "You ain't seen nothin' yet, big boy. Wait'll they get you out on that field this afternoon! They're sure plottin' somethin'."

POOR SPORTSMANSHIP

"They're always plottin'," growled Soapy.

"Yeah," continued Pop, "they're up to somethin'. Been up in the office all afternoon with big cards. They were up there all mornin' too."

"Probably making up the plays," said Chip. His eyes wandered past Pop and up to the wall. High above the lockers, some of Coach Rockwell's sayings and slogans adorned the white wall.

A TEAM THAT WON'T BE BEAT—CAN'T BE BEAT.

IF YOU DON'T PLAY TO WIN— WHY KEEP SCORE?

Chip's jaw set grimly as he bent down again to finish lacing his shoes.

"Grass drill!" bawled Soapy. "I thought a grass drill was somethin' to plant grass seed with."

"Here they come," someone said.

Seconds later, Coach Rockwell descended the short flight of steps leading down from the gymnasium. "Never mind your shoes, boys," he called. "Come up here in the gym for a 'skull session,' a little strategy session before practice." He turned and clumped back up the stairs.

"Skull practice," groaned Soapy. "Better have his *own* skull examined!"

"He'd have to use a drill to get through that skull of yours," someone said.

"Yeah!" Soapy retorted. "A *Rock* drill! Guess you won't have to worry about bein' magna laudna."

"*Magna cum laude,* you clown," said Chip.

"Yeah," mimicked Soapy. "Lodna, podna, modna . . . Whatever!"

TOUCHDOWN PASS

In a short time, the whole squad was gathered in the gymnasium stands. Coach Rockwell paced back and forth in front of the portable whiteboard with short, nervous steps. His black eyes were snapping more than usual; everything about him expressed concentration on football. Every boy sensed this session was important. The Rock was up to something, and he was excited about it.

The Valley Falls gymnasium and physical education facilities were modern in every respect. J. P. Ohlsen, devoted Valley Falls civic leader, had helped sponsor expansion of the high school athletic plant. Located in the back of the high school, it occupied an entire wing and housed a basketball complex with seating facilities for three thousand spectators. The red-brick building included another gym, a swimming pool, a number of physical education teaching stations, and the athletic offices. North of the wing, covering a whole block, was the athletic field. An eight-lane, red-and-white, all-weather track circled Ohlsen Stadium, and the concrete stands could seat five thousand fans.

"Now, while we're resting," began Coach Rockwell, "we'll discuss offensive play. We made up our minds last night, boys, that we're going to play from the T and some special Valley Falls variations of the T-formation."

The suddenness and seriousness of the announcement shocked every player to instant attention.

"Now, how do you feel about the T-formation?" Coach Rockwell's black eyes were looking directly at Chip Hilton.

"Well, Coach, we all know you've been trying us out, shifting us around and trying to figure out what we could handle best, and I, well, I—"

"What?"

"I think we could handle the T best!"

Coach Rockwell suddenly tossed the ball he had been holding into Biggie Cohen's hands. If he had expected to catch the big tackle by surprise, he was disappointed. Biggie's ham-like hands closed over the brown leather ball swiftly and surely.

"What do you think, Biggie?"

"I like the T, Coach." Biggie was clearly nervous.

"Why?"

"Umm—like Chip says, it seems to me we'd be better with it, Coach."

Coach Rockwell saved Biggie further embarrassment by motioning for the ball. He turned to Williams.

"You're one of the regulars, Ted. How do you feel about using the T?"

The tall, quiet senior hesitated a second and then answered slowly, "I agree with Chip, Coach. Personally, I'd rather use the double wing, but I don't think we have the squad for it. I do think, however, that we have the speed for the T."

Soapy Smith impulsively blurted out, "The T fits Speed to a tee!"

Coach Rockwell swung slowly about and regarded Soapy intently. Soapy slid down in his seat and dropped his chin. His face flamed to a brighter red than usual, and he gulped twice, quickly. After a tense second, a flicker of a smile played along the edges of Coach Rockwell's lips. "You've got something there, Soapy," he chuckled.

Soapy breathed something about "my big mouth," and gave an audible sigh of relief.

Coach Rockwell nodded toward Coaches Thomas and Stewart.

TOUCHDOWN PASS

"Well, boys, my two bosses here have been talking nothing but the T-formation since the first day of practice. It isn't the T-formation itself that makes for a successful system. It's the type of player that makes the system.

"The clever, speedy player has a greater chance with the T because it's based on finesse. Feinting, maneuvering, and then striking with speed and deception. We just happen to have more players this year who can fit into the T and fewer who could be used successfully in the double wing or the other offenses we explored.

"The T is the oldest formation in football and one of the best. Handled properly, it's strong inside the tackles and, with a man in motion, effective outside the ends. Furthermore, it's a good passing formation and ideal for quick-opening plays."

He turned to the whiteboard and outlined the formation.

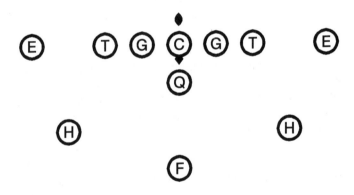

"That's the way we'll use the T. Balanced line, ends loose, fullback four and a half yards back of the ball, halfbacks four yards back of the line and off the tackle's outside shoulder, quarterback directly back of the center."

POOR SPORTSMANSHIP

"That big circle on the left is Biggie," Soapy whispered dramatically.

Coach Rockwell spent the next half-hour outlining and discussing the basic plays of the T-formation. After that, he ordered the squad out onto the field to run signals. The players were excited and hurriedly laced on their shoes; they wanted to try out the T.

"All right, boys," the Rock said finally, "we'll have a little scrimmage. Team A and Team B. Team A on the offense first down on their own forty-yard line. Bill, you watch Team B. I'll follow Team A. Everyone in helmets. Let's go!"

Jordan called, "Signals! Chip on a cross buck over right tackle. On two! Let's go!"

Chip didn't focus his eyes on the hole, but out of the corner of one eye he noted Fats Ohlsen's defensive position. "Pile on this time, fat stuff," he muttered half aloud.

Jordan took the pass from Trullo on the count of two, faked to Williams, and plunked the ball in Chip's belly as he drove forward with all his strength. Just as he got to the line, Chip saw an opening to the left and started to cut back. As he did so, Fats Ohlsen lunged to his right, and Chip let him have a powerful straight-arm. The big boy dropped flat on his face as Chip plowed forward.

"That's one for me," Chip muttered as he scrambled to his feet seven yards ahead. He was off the ground almost before the whistle shrilled and back in the huddle. He liked this! Fats Ohlsen wanted action—he'd get it!

"Let me have it again, Jordan. Same play!"

"OK, Chip. Same play, guys. Snap on one. Break!"

Again, Jordan faked the ball to Williams and handed the ball to Chip, who drove full speed right over Ohlsen's position.

This time, Chip faked a cutback, dropped his right shoulder, and then bowled Ohlsen over with a forceful shoulder smash into his stomach. As Fats went down, Chip pivoted and cut down the sideline for twenty yards before he was brought down by Cody Collins.

Benjamin "Biggie" Cohen had taken care of Badger on the play. He had barely cross-checked Ohlsen before meeting Badger head-on. No one met Biggie Cohen head-on and kept his feet! Badger was shaking the cobwebs out of his head and resting on one knee when Cohen reached a big hand down and lifted him to his feet.

"Sorry, pal." He grinned. "Just part of the game."

Back in the huddle an elated Chip slapped Cohen on the back. "Nice blocking, Biggie," he said. "That'll hold *him!*"

"Guess that'll hold Ohlsen too," whispered Ted Williams. "Look!"

Ohlsen was down on both knees in his tackle position. He was still trying to get his breath and a trickle of red flowed from his swollen nose.

"Give it to him again," said Biggie grimly.

Chip shook his head. "No, that's enough. Let's play! All right! We're getting an offense at last!"

Jordan hollered, "Signals," and the players gathered around him in the huddle. "I'll try a pass to Speed," he whispered. "Speed in motion toward the right on the count of two—ball on five. Let's go, guys! Break!"

Trullo snapped the ball to Jordan on the count of five, and Jordan Taylor cut behind Chip for a position to pass to Speed out in the right flat. Chip dumped the defensive left end who had charged in and immediately regained his feet. Just then he heard a shout from behind and Coach Rockwell's whistle killing the play. He turned to see Jordan lying flat on his back where he had been thoroughly dumped by the defensive right end. Someone had missed a blocking assignment.

As Chip stood there, completely relaxed, a heavy body struck him viciously in the back of the knees, and he was conscious of a sharp pain in his right leg as he sank to the ground. He tried to regain his feet, but his legs wouldn't hold his weight. They felt paralyzed. As he slumped back into a sitting position on the ground, he saw Nick Trullo and Chris Badger grinning.

Fats Ohlsen scrambled to his feet. "How'd you like that treatment, Chippy?" he sneered.

Chip dug both hands in the ground and made a mighty effort to get up, but there was no strength in his legs.

Coach Rockwell was shaking with anger. He spun Ohlsen around. "Didn't you hear the whistle?" he demanded tersely.

"Sure I heard it, but I couldn't stop," Ohlsen replied sullenly.

"That's not true," said Coach Rockwell. "You clipped Hilton fully five seconds after the whistle. That's dirty football! That's not the first time you've shown poor sportsmanship out here, Ohlsen, but it's the last time!"

He turned to Coach Thomas. "Take him in to Pop, Bill. Check in his equipment. I won't have that kind of football around here nor that kind of player. Football's rough, but we play a clean game and by the rules!"

Ohlsen glowered at the ground. Then he cast a malicious glance at Chip and, with head down, slowly trudged toward the end of the field. Coach Rockwell watched Ohlsen's deliberate progress off the field and then turned to Hilton. "You better go in and let Pop look at that leg,

Chip." He motioned to Stewart. "Take Hilton to the dressing room, Chet." He turned to the startled squad. "All right, let's go. Take Hilton's place at fullback, Badger. You get over here and call the plays, Collins."

The solicitous trainer soon had Hilton up on the trainer's table in the dressing room. As Pop massaged his legs, Chip could hear Ohlsen out in the locker room slamming his locker and muttering to himself. Chip's legs were still numb.

"That'll wear off, Chip," Pop said reassuringly. "The muscles might stiffen up a bit, but you'll be OK in a couple of days. It's just like a bad charley horse in your thigh. I'll drop down to the Sugar Bowl tonight and see how you're doin'. OK?"

Chip limped into the locker room and, sinking down on the bench in front of his locker, relaxed gratefully. Ohlsen was waiting for this opportunity. Coach Thomas and Chet Stewart had returned to the field. Here was his chance.

Pop had noted the sudden silence in the locker room and barely had time to call out as Ohlsen struck. The warning was too late; Chip never even heard it. Slipping behind the unsuspecting Hilton, Fats launched a savage blow that landed smack under Chip's right eye. Ohlsen's cheap shot knocked Chip to the floor, completely bewildered.

Fats followed up his advantage. He jumped down on Hilton with both knees and pummeled him with both fists. Chip tried desperately to gain his feet, but Fats had him securely pinned. He could only grab Ohlsen's arms and hang on, playing for time.

Pop tried to pull Fats off Chip, but the big boy was too heavy. He couldn't budge him. Just then the squad swarmed into the dressing room, and Pop shouted for help.

POOR SPORTSMANSHIP

"What's going on here?" Biggie Cohen bellowed. He charged down the narrow locker room aisle like a wild bull and lifted Fats off Chip as if he were a mere cover. Biggie was raging mad. He pinned Ohlsen against the lockers and banged Fats's head as if he were shaking a rag doll. It took every ounce of strength on the part of Coach Thomas and Coach Stewart to pull Cohen away. A moment later, Coach Rockwell's angry voice overpowered the confusion.

"Clear this dressing room. Now! Everybody back on the field. Get 'em out of here, Chet!" He stood glaring from Hilton to Ohlsen. "Fighting? All right. You're both through! Turn in your uniform too, Hilton!"

Thirty minutes later a worried Speed Morris tried to cheer up a brooding Chip as they drove home in the unusually silent Mustang. "What happened? Quit worryin'. He isn't worth it! Everyone knows Ohlsen's not a team player. He's no good. Coach'll take you back."

But all of Speed's efforts were in vain. Chip Hilton wasn't talking.

CHAPTER 4

On the Carpet

CHIP HILTON stood in front of the mirror in his room looking at a very black eye. All night he had tossed and turned. What was going to happen at school today? Well, he'd have to face it. His legs were stiff, but he wasn't going to limp, even if it killed him.

Speed and Biggie met him on his way up the long flight of steps, and, shoulder to shoulder, solidarity in motion, the three boys walked down the corridor to their homeroom. Joel Ohlsen was surrounded by a group of students just inside the big door; excited talk about the fight buzzed through every Valley Falls hallway.

Chip scarcely heard a thing that was said in his classes all day. His mind was filled with his suspension from the team. He didn't know whether to go out to the field to watch practice or not. It required a supreme effort when three o'clock rolled around not to follow the crowd to the stadium. Instead, he headed slowly to the Sugar Bowl. Walking down the busy street, Chip flexed his leg muscles; he was still sore. All day in school he had been subjected to sly glances and smothered giggles when the other students noticed his eye. Isolated and embarrassed, Chip felt as if the whole school was staring at him.

"Fats Ohlsen whipped Chip Hilton!" That's what they were all thinking and saying. Well, wait until the next time. He wouldn't get ambushed again. Next time Joel wanted to tangle, he'd be prepared for that first lick. Fats was too slow. All he had to do was to keep away from a clinch, keep jabbing for a while and then hook his face with a hard right . . . just once . . . just once.

Mr. Schroeder greeted him understandingly. "Well, looks like you had a bit of trouble!" He gripped Chip's shoulder affectionately. "Don't let it get you down. I heard Joel Ohlsen badgering and baiting you out front last night, and I want you to know I admired your self-control. It takes a lot of courage to endure the badgering of a bully!"

He scanned Chip's face carefully for a second and then continued grimly, "From what I can gather, you got the best of him on the field, and he couldn't take it. I'd just continue to ignore him. That completely upsets a bully." He waited expectantly, but Chip remained silent.

"Oh, by the way, J. P. said George Browning is nearly all set for a job. His papers looked good. Tell him to report to Jonathan Kim at the pottery employment office tomorrow morning at eight o'clock. J. P. said something about needing an experienced man in the mixing department. If his meeting goes well, then he's in business. Chip, you know, it's too bad Joel isn't like his father. J. P. Ohlsen is one of the finest men to ever live in this town."

TOUCHDOWN PASS

In spite of the good news about Mr. Browning, sleep that night again was impossible, and it was a tired Chip Hilton who was summoned to the principal's office after English class the next morning. Mr. Zimmerman motioned Chip toward a chair. "Sit down, Hilton," he said kindly.

Coach Rockwell; Mr. Rogers, the athletic director; Pop; and Joel Ohlsen were seated in the room, all facing the principal's large oak desk. "I guess we're all here, Coach," Zimmerman said. "You go right ahead now, and let's see if we can settle this situation."

Rockwell wasted no time. "Chip, we've been talking about you and Joel, here. Mr. Zimmerman has called us together to see if we can't do something about this long-standing feud between you two boys. I don't know what started this affair, and I'm not the least bit interested. However, you boys certainly can't go through your whole lives fighting each other, and I, for one, would like to see you two forget the whole thing.

"Football's a pretty good medium for getting rid of the fight urge, and, for the life of me, I don't know why you can't get rid of your excess energy that way. How about shaking hands and calling this whole thing to an end? How about it, Hilton? How about it, Ohlsen?"

Chip's face was flushed but his gray eyes were steady as they met those of the coach. He deliberated a moment and then cast a swift glance at Ohlsen.

"It's all right with me, Coach," he said slowly. "I'm willing to shake hands."

Rockwell turned to Ohlsen. "How about you, Joel?"

Joel Ohlsen's face remained sullen. He shook his head stubbornly. "I don't want to shake his hand."

"Why not?"

"I just don't want to, that's why."

ON THE CARPET

"You mean you don't want to play football bad enough to forget a trivial elementary school argument?"

"I want to play football, but I don't want to shake hands with Hilton!"

Principal Zimmerman addressed Coach Rockwell. "Excuse me, Hank, for interrupting." He leaned forward and smiled patiently at Ohlsen.

"Joel, life's too short to carry a grudge around in your heart. There are too many important things for young men like you to think about." He gestured toward Rogers and Rockwell. "I can't believe you have failed to develop an understanding of sportsmanship in your schooling and athletics here at Valley Falls High School. I just can't!"

Zimmerman's voice was gently persuasive as he continued, "Come on, Joel, let's all shake hands and forget it. What do you say?"

Joel's eyes were intently focused on the floor, and he shook his head obstinately. "I'll *never* shake hands with that Hilton!"

Zimmerman leaned back in his chair resignedly. "All right, Joel," he said coldly. "That's all. You may go now."

Ohlsen stood up slowly. "What about football?" he asked defiantly.

"I'm afraid there's no place for that kind of attitude on our squad, Joel," Rockwell said quietly.

"Fine. That's OK by me!"

"All right, young man. That's all."

Joel shrugged and stepped toward the door, throwing Chip one last contemptuous sneer.

"Thanks for coming, Pop," Rockwell smiled gratefully and then turned to Hilton. "Chip, Pop told us about Ohlsen striking you from behind. Sorry I didn't know that at the time."

TOUCHDOWN PASS

The hard lines on Rockwell's chiseled face relaxed. "Must be a little rough walking around with that colorful shiner. But I guess you can take it!"

Chip smiled ruefully. "Guess I'll have to, Coach," he said.

"That's the spirit! See you at practice!"

That afternoon after school, Joel Ohlsen and Donald "Wheels" Ferris sauntered slowly down the long school steps and then turned down Main Street. As they reached the corner where Ohlsen always turned to go up the hill toward his large, stately house and Wheels turned down toward the pottery, they stopped to talk. Joel told Wheels about the Zimmerman meeting. He was in a bitter mood.

Ever since grade school days, Ohlsen had found it difficult to make and hold friends, chiefly because he had shown off his father's wealth and prestige at every opportunity. Not that J. P. Ohlsen wasn't a man of whom any fellow or town could be proud. J. P. was respected by everyone.

One of the most influential people in Valley Falls, Joel's father was president of the Valley Falls Pottery and an extensive property owner. He took an active interest in civic administration and was keenly engaged in the welfare and well-being of all Valley Falls citizens. Everyone knew, liked, and respected him. Not so his son. Those who endured Joel Jr. usually did so because they hoped to benefit through his position as J. P.'s son.

Wheels wasn't feeling any too comfortable with Joel's anger. He wanted to change the subject.

"Goin' down to Mike's?" he ventured.

"No, I'm not going down to Mike's!" Ohlsen snapped, deep in thought.

ON THE CARPET

Wheels and Joel were a strange pair. Wheels had been on Joel's side for a long time and, although he didn't always agree with everything Joel did, was glad to have him for a friend. The Ferris family had fallen on hard times, and Joel brought Wheels a little closer to luxuries and conveniences his family couldn't afford. Joel had a car and all the money he needed. He was a free spender, too, especially when he was trying to show off to someone. But there was something deeper. Donald Ferris also felt kind of sorry for Joel. He didn't really have anybody else. Wheels knew how that felt.

Ohlsen had tried hard to impress the athletes. This was the one group he most wanted to join. So far, he had met with little success; with the exception of Badger and Collins, the rest ignored him completely. In desperation, he had gone out for football. That was all ended now. Joel actually didn't feel too bad about it; he'd been about ready to quit anyway. He couldn't see the reason for those long hours of practice and, as for training, that was completely out of the question. He was too interested in smoking and keeping late hours down near the flats, the industrial section of town. And he liked sliding through the side door of the Academy into Mike Sorelli's poolroom.

Academy Bowling was one of the more popular locations for recreation in Valley Falls. The facility contained thirty bowling lanes, a snack bar, and a video game room. During the week, adult bowling leagues dominated the lanes. Saturday mornings were reserved for the Junior League. Special events and couples reigned on Saturday nights. The game room was most crowded on Saturday mornings before and after the Juniors.

Tucked in a far corner of the Academy was Sorelli's Pool and Billiards. Chiefly the younger pottery workers, the customers worked hard and played hard. Occasionally, a few businessmen and delivery men finished off their lunch hours shooting a few friendly racks of pool. However, the room also attracted a negative element. Several sleazy-looking men hung out at Mike's and never seemed to work at any real jobs—but always had money.

There were lots of stories told about gambling that originated at Mike's but was carried out somewhere else. Sorelli was too clever to run these customers off, but he was also too concerned about his business to allow anything illegal to take place in the room.

Coach Rockwell was bitter and vehement in his denunciation of Sorelli's. He called it a "dive" and warned his athletes to stay away from the place.

Wheels broke the silence. "Say, Joel—"

"Yeah?" Ohlsen was impatient. "What?"

"What if you and Hilton did have a fight? Guys fight and then everything's OK after they've gotten it off their chests."

"Well, not me!" growled Ohlsen.

"Look, Joel," Wheels continued, "you know that Hilton, Morris, Biggie Cohen, Red Schwartz, and all the athletes stick pretty much together—"

"So what if they do!"

"Nothin'. Only I—I think it would be smarter to be friends with that crowd. Most everybody thinks they're all right."

"Well, nobody's holding you back!" challenged Ohlsen.

"Aw, Joel, I wasn't talking about me. I meant you." Wheels hesitated. "Whatever you do is all right with me, but I still think those guys are OK."

"Yeah? Well, Hilton and his crew will be sorry when I get finished with them!"

CHAPTER 5

Coffin Corner

"NICE SHOT!"

Chip recovered the basketball and turned toward the direction of the voice. George Browning Sr. was leaning against the fence which bounded the east side of the Hilton A.C.

"Thanks, Mr. Browning." Chip smiled self-consciously. "It's easy to make 'em when no one is guarding you."

Chip shifted the basketball from one hand to the other and moved toward the fence. He was just a bit stiff from the afternoon's football practice. A few minutes of basketball was just the thing to loosen up tight muscles.

George Browning cleared his throat. "Chip," he said hesitantly, "I want to thank you and Mr. Schroeder for opening the door to my new job. I appreciate it, Chip."

"Oh, thanks, Mr. Browning, but Mr. Schroeder did it."

"I know, Chip, but you asked Mr. Schroeder to do it. I want you to know how grateful I am."

A strong bond had already developed between George Browning and Chip. They had talked several times before over the backyard fence and Chip had warmed to George Sr. just as he had to Taps.

"How do you like the new job?" Chip asked.

"Fine, Chip. But pottery work isn't new to me, you know. I've been working in clay all my life. This job though, thanks to you and Mr. Schroeder, is probably the best I've ever had. I've been in charge of mixing departments before, but this facility is tops."

The two were still talking when Mary Hilton called Chip for dinner. As they shared their meal, Chip told his mother about the session in the principal's office. Mary Hilton's intent gray eyes met and held Chip's.

"You've had a rough couple of days, Chip. I'm proud of you for offering your hand to Joel. I think that boy could use a friend like you."

"Thanks, Mom, but I don't think Joel would think so." Chip ruefully shook his head. "I just don't understand Joel. I'm sure glad it's over though, and Coach Rockwell knows what really happened."

The conversation turned to the afternoon's practice. "We're going out to Midwestern tomorrow afternoon, Mom, for a scrimmage. That'll be my first real chance at fullback. I've *got* to make good tomorrow!"

"You will. You'll give it your best, I know. Hurry home after work. You'll get a good night's rest now that this is all settled with Coach Rockwell. How about taking the car for a fill-up on your way home?"

Mary Hilton was deeply concerned about Joel Ohlsen's antagonism toward Chip. But she knew better than to press Chip for all the details; little by little, the whole story would come out.

Time dragged for Chip that night at the Sugar Bowl and at school the next day. Three o'clock finally came though, and Chip raced for the dressing room. He and Speed hustled out to the field. But the others were not far behind, and soon the whole squad was assembled around Rockwell and a tall, white-haired stranger.

"Boys," began Rockwell, "we haven't much time. The bus will be here any minute to take us out to Midwestern. Unfortunately, this is the only day Tug Watson could be here so he'll be coming along with us. Some of you remember, I'm sure, last year when Tug came out here and helped Tim Murphy and a couple of others with their kicking. Tug knows more about kicking a football than anyone alive, and you kickers can learn a lot from him."

The boys looked at the famous All-American with respect that came close to being awe.

"I hope I can still *lift* a football, to say nothing about booting it, when I'm that guy's age!" muttered Soapy Smith.

"There's the bus," Zach Harris shouted.

The whole squad broke for the bright yellow bus as one man, whooping and yelling. They had looked forward to this scrimmage with Coach Alvin Hoffman's squad for the past two weeks. Keen competition had always existed between Valley Falls High School and Midwestern, a private boarding school. At one time regular games in all sports had been scheduled, but the games had gotten out of hand; the rivalry had become too keen. Now, the only chance they had to compete was in seasonal scrimmages.

TOUCHDOWN PASS

Midwestern Preparatory School was located five miles from Valley Falls in the little town of Plains. Unlike Valley Falls, Plains was little more than a crossroads with a post office, a store or two, and a few houses. However, the Midwestern grounds and buildings were spread out on both sides of Valley Turnpike and gave Plains the appearance of a small town.

The bus took the turn at Midwestern's main gate a little too fast and spattered the bluestone gravel on the lawns fronting both sides of the winding driveway.

"Sacrilege!" Soapy hollered. "Sacrilege! That's what it is! Dirtying up that bee-u-tee-ful landscape."

"Yeah?" Red Schwartz yelled. "Just wait! Wait'll you see what Valley Falls does to these pretty-boy preppies!"

"Fawncy that!" quipped Soapy just before his teammates chimed in with a raucous chorus of comments and laughter.

"Quite right, old chap, quite right!"

"Oh, do-ooo pardon our frequent and numerous touchdowns!"

"I simply *must* polish my football shoes—my valet has forgotten his duties again!"

"Is my hair stunning?"

"Yes, it's per-fect-ly horrid!"

"I am *so* ashamed—there's a hole in my sock exposing my little toe."

"Tragic, old man, simply tragic!"

"Do keep a stiff upper lip!"

Valley Falls athletes had always ribbed the wealthy private school students like this. Yet, they were well aware that some of the best athletes in the country had gotten their start at Midwestern. Its teams were tough and had always been ready for Valley Falls.

COFFIN CORNER

The Midwestern Royals were running through drills when the bus pulled to a stop, and they paused and stood watching the Big Reds pile out onto the field. Pop Brown and Chet Stewart carried the bench equipment and a bag of balls to one side of the field. Coach Rockwell and Tug Watson walked over to talk with Coach Hoffman.

"Step on it!" snapped Coach Thomas. "Let's go! Don't stand there gawking. Circle out for team warm-ups."

Chet Stewart sent Chip, Soapy Smith, and Jordan Taylor over next to the Midwestern bleachers with Tug Watson.

"The punt is a powerful weapon. The punter's defensive team depends on him to move the ball deep inside their opponents' territory. A well-placed punt gives a distinct edge to the defense," instructed Tug.

Watson assigned Soapy to the job of snapping the ball back from the center position and sent Jordan down the sideline to recover the kicks.

"Now, Hilton," Watson said, "let me see how you punt. Center the ball, Smith."

Chip caught the ball, took a long stride forward with his right leg, followed with a step on his left, and then gave the ball a resounding thump with his right foot. The ball sailed down the field in a perfect spiral.

"That's a nice kick, Chip. You've got a lot of drive in that leg of yours, kiddo. But you didn't have much height or hang time. A high kick allows good coverage by your ends. Then, they have time to get downfield and tackle the receiver before he can get started. Let's try it my way, once."

Tug Watson showed Chip how to hold the ball with his left hand and guide it with his right. He urged Chip to hold the ball a little higher and not drop it too soon. Then he worked on Chip's footwork, making him take a relaxed position with his left foot advanced. As the ball came back, he showed Chip how to take a short back step with his left foot, catch the ball, and then take a short step forward with the right foot. Then, a full step with the left, and the kick and follow-through with the right foot.

Chip soon learned how to rock back on his left foot and meet the ball with his right foot; the rocker motion seemed to add power to his kicks too. He noticed, also, that when he used the rocker, he wasn't ending up so close to the line of scrimmage. That would eliminate a bit of the danger of a blocked kick by the opponents.

Chip finally caught hold of one; it drilled high in the air and then nosed down toward the ground with unbelievable speed.

Soapy's mouth fell open in astonishment. "What a boot!" he gasped. "That's the best kick I ever saw. Sure got hold of that one, didn't he, Mr. Watson?"

"That was a beauty, Soapy. Nice hang time, Chip."

"I guess it was an accident," Chip offered modestly.

"That was no accident," Tug Watson said firmly. "You just practice the rocker I showed you and finish with your foot high over your head, and there won't be any accidents—or bad kicks either!"

Time after time, Chip punted the ball accurately. His leg was still a little sore and stiff, but he felt a thrill because deep within his heart he knew he hadn't really met that ball with all his power. Wait until he could really open up and give it all he had.

There was a familiar-sounding thump out on the field and the chug of running cleats. Tug Watson and Chip turned to watch.

The Midwestern fullback, standing on his own thirty-yard line, had booted a long, low punt to Speed clear down on the Big Reds' twenty. It was a solid fifty-yard punt, but there was no one near Speed when he gathered in the ball. He ran straight up the field to Valley Falls's forty-five-yard line before he was downed.

Chip turned to find Tug Watson's bright blue eyes regarding him quizzically.

"I get it!" Chip exclaimed excitedly. "I see it now! A fifty-yard punt ends up with a net gain of twenty-five yards—really only fifteen yards from the point of the previous down."

"Right, but only because it wasn't high enough to give the Midwestern ends time to get down to cover the receiver," added Watson.

Watson gestured to Soapy to cover the ball. "All right, now, Hilton, we'll try some out-of-bounds kicks; we'll kick a few into the coffin corner. Now, Chip, coffin-corner kicking is extremely important. Every college punter in the country spends hours on coffin-corner kicking. It's that important!

"Any team that has to keep starting their offense from the shadow of their goal gets the jitters and their opponents usually get the breaks.

"There are two kinds of out-of-bounds kicks. First, there's the kick you can use when you're past midfield and you want to rifle the ball all the way out in the air—usually a spiral. Then, there's the end-over-end kick when you're back in your own half of the field.

"We'll assume that line roller down there is the ten-yard marker and that last bench is the goal line. Now, try to kick the ball out of bounds between the marker and the bench."

Chip's first kick went straight over the roller. Several times the ball sailed over the bench, but most of the time it held a line from the point where he was kicking to a spot between the roller and the bench.

"That's nice kicking, Hilton. You've got natural kicking ability," Watson patted Chip on the back.

"Now, we're going to move back fifteen or twenty yards, and I want you to try an end-over-end kick. Careful, now, you've got to meet the ball squarely with the toe, slightly above the center—you can't use your instep on this kick—meet it with the toe and aim at a spot on the field where you want it to hit the ground. It isn't a very high kick; it just clears the line, in fact. Now try the first one easy and aim the ball right down there toward the line roller again."

Chip met the ball just as Tug Watson had instructed. Kick after kick, he sent the ball driving down the field in a straight line. It landed on the ground and went end over end right for the roller or the bench. The ball went fast too.

Watson was pleased. When he and Chip finished the practice, they walked over to the bench. "OK, Rock," Watson said, smacking Chip on the back. "Here's the kicker you're looking for."

A little later, Rockwell sent Chip, Jordan Taylor, and Soapy Smith in for Badger, Collins, and Trullo.

"Play a kicking game," he said. "See if you can gain on your punt exchanges."

Watson's coaching really paid off! Chip outpunted the Midwestern fullback again and again. Gradually the exchange of kicks forced Midwestern back to their own goal line. Chip's last kick was a beauty; he drilled a coffin-corner boot out of bounds on the Midwestern three-yard line.

"What happened to you?" Speed quizzed in the huddle.

"Yeah, and what have you been holding back on us for?" Biggie challenged.

"Mr. Watson gave me some good pointers. Did you notice the difference?"

"Radical!" confirmed Speed, a wide grin breaking across his face.

It was a leg-weary athlete that Speed Morris nudged out of his three-speed fastback in front of the Hilton home two hours later. Taps Browning was sitting on the front steps, and he greeted Chip happily. "Hi ya, Chip, how'd the game go?"

"Team looked good. I'm worn out, but it feels good. What are you lookin' so pleased about?"

"Oh, everything. Just everything! Everything's great since Dad went to work. We sure appreciate what you did, Chip. Mom's so happy!"

"Skip it. C'mon, let's shoot a few. How about some hoops? We'll play to twenty-one."

After dinner, Taps went down to the Sugar Bowl with Chip. They followed their usual route—down Beech to Main and then south past the Academy Bowling Center.

Just as Chip and Taps arrived in front of the Academy, Joel Ohlsen appeared in the side doorway of Sorelli's. Chip was puzzled to see Fats suddenly dart back into the poolroom. But the reason for the boy's strange behavior was soon apparent—J. P. Ohlsen's sleek, black Cadillac was gliding swiftly down the street.

No wonder Fats ducked back! Chip thought. J. P. Ohlsen was a stern man, yet Fats seemed to be able to pull the wool completely over his father's eyes . . . in more ways than one.

CHAPTER 6

Coach on the Field

THE VIBRANT strains of the "Valley Falls School March" wafted through the open windows of the gymnasium. Out on the field, the school band, dressed in red-and-white capes and uniforms, paraded before the rapidly filling stadium stands.

Chip and Speed sat side by side in the dressing room, furiously lacing up their cleats. When the players finished dressing, they climbed the stairs to the gymnasium. This was the day of the Hampton game. The football players were excited and filled with opening-day jitters. They wanted out on that field!

Speed winked at Chip and grinned. "This is it, buddy!" he said. "Man, oh man, this *is* the day."

In the big gym, the players were assembled on the bleachers. Game days were the only days Coach Rockwell permitted football cleats on the edge of the gymnasium floor and only then with special care. The boys even tip-toed across the rubberized floor runner, being careful not to step on the sacred, waxed hardwood floor, and seated themselves in front of the whiteboard.

Coach Rockwell was half-sitting on a little table, and Bill Thomas and Chet Stewart were standing nearby, talking quietly. Soapy referred to these team meetings as "more of the Rock's skull sessions."

Pop and Dink Davis came pumping up the stairs. Dink, voted the most spirited Valley Falls student, led the student cheering section. Following Valley Falls tradition, the captain of the team was elected just before the first game of the season. Dink was eager to carry the results of the election out to the stadium so the fans could recognize the new captain as he led the team onto the field.

"All set, Coach," Pop breathed. "Everybody's out."

Coach Rockwell was serious. "All right now, boys, let's have a little quiet. This is our first game, and so it's the day we elect a captain to lead us out on the field and into a new season. Chet, suppose you and Bill each take a marker and act as recorders. Got paper and pencils, Pop? Good! Pass them out!

"Now, boys, remember, selecting a captain is an important matter. A good captain is a coach on the field. He must be able to accept responsibilities and make decisions. Don't vote for someone just because he's your friend. Choose someone who will make a good leader and serve the team.

"All right, let's have the votes. Remember, one vote, one count, that's all. There's no second voting. Make it snappy! Keep your vote to yourself. Collect the votes, Pop."

Chip quickly wrote "Morris" and handed the slip of paper to Pop. Then, while he waited, he considered the candidates. There were only four letter men. Speed, Biggie, Ted, and himself. Of the four, only Ted Williams was a senior. Speed, Biggie, and he were juniors. *Ted might get it. He would be good. Boy, what an honor! I wish . . .*

"It'll be Speed, though," he whispered half-aloud. Soon all the slips of paper were piled on the little table. Pop glanced at each one as he handed the slips of paper to Coach Rockwell who called out the names.

The first vote was for Morris; so were the second and the third. The next vote was for Hilton. Chip's ears burned. Then came two votes for Badger and one for Soapy Smith.

"Who did that?" Soapy snarled belligerently, but grinning as he looked from one player to another.

"Humph," groaned Red Schwartz. "Sure! As if you didn't know."

Three votes were tallied for Biggie Cohen and one for Williams. Another for Williams, and then four in a row for Hilton. Chip's heart was pounding. Two were called for Badger and two more for Morris.

Chip looked at the marks on the whiteboard. Speed and he were tied. He swallowed hard and looked down at his cleated shoes. Why was the coach going so *slowly*?

"Morris . . . Hilton . . . Morris . . . Morris . . . Hilton . . . Cohen . . . Morris."

In spite of all Chip's attempts to shut out Coach Rockwell's voice, his mind kept count. He wanted this honor more than he had ever wanted anything. Unable to stand the suspense any longer, he glanced at the board.

Morris had nine votes; Hilton had seven. Biggie Cohen and Chuck Badger each had four, Ted Williams two, and Soapy Smith one. Now, only two pieces of paper remained. Well, that put Speed in.

Pop gingerly opened the last two little pieces of paper. A wide grin spread over his face as he handed them to the coach. Coach Rockwell smiled and handed one to Chet Stewart and one to Bill Thomas. The eyes of every boy in the room were on the two coaches.

Bill Thomas quickly drew a line under Hilton's name. All eyes were on Chet Stewart now. He turned a little and his glance met Chip's. Chip sensed it—a tie vote! *It's gonna be Speed and me.*

Stewart pivoted and raised his hand. Before he even made the mark, a roar of cheers greeted the end of the vote. Valley Falls had co-captains for the season!

Coach Rockwell motioned to Chip and Speed and thrust out a hand to each player. "Congratulations, boys, you deserve the honor." He turned to the seated team. "Boys, here are your captains. Let's hope they lead us to a successful season."

Whoops, cheers, whistles, and rounds of high-fives broke the pregame tension until Coach Rockwell silenced them. "Team," he said, "this is it! It's been a long, tough road of drills and rough workouts, but we're here. Now go out there and give 'em all you've got!" He stepped back slowly as Chip and Speed joined hands and the squad gathered around them. Each player wanted to be part of that sports gesture that signifies team spirit. Chip turned and caught Coach Rockwell's eye. Impulsively, he reached out a hand and pulled the coach into the group. Now, at least for one little second, they were all pulling together.

With a cheering squad of teammates following, Chip and Speed broke out of the gym door and matched stride for stride as they led the squad through the stadium gate and onto the field. Dink Davis and his cheering squad led a tremendous crowd cheer as the band blasted out the "Valley Falls Victory March."

"HILTON—RAH! RAH—RAH—HILTON!
MORRIS—RAH! RAH—RAH—MORRIS!
R—A—H! VALLEY FALLS!
GO BIG RED! GO BIG RED!"

The squads separated quickly for warm-up drills and after a few minutes gathered around Coach Rockwell in front of the bench. As Rockwell began giving final details, a roar from the other side of the stadium announced the Hampton squad's entrance onto the field. All the Big Reds craned their necks to check out their opponents. They looked big in their flashy, light-orange-colored jerseys with bold black numbers.

The sharp ring of Rockwell's voice snapped them around again. "All right, boys, line up in your units—Red, White, and VF. Just as you were yesterday afternoon."

Something too big for his chest seemed to be choking Chip. He'd wanted to start today; last year he'd been just another end and had started every game. This year he was co-captain and was sitting the bench. He'd have been better off at his old position.

As Chip joined the second team, Soapy Smith slapped him on the back. There was a look of understanding in Soapy's blue eyes. "The thick, old blockhead," he growled. "Seems like he could've started you—you are only the captain!"

Chip grinned. "Somebody's got to captain you guys on the bench," he said. Suddenly the ache in his chest and the lump in his throat were gone. His mind was clear. He was co-captain of the Valley Falls football team. Starting the game meant nothing. Everybody couldn't start. He'd be in there soon. Somebody had to sit the bench. His teammates had confidence in him; that was the important thing. He wouldn't let them down. He'd play his head off . . . when he got in.

Chris Badger, Speed, and Chip were alternating with practice punts. Chip warmed up slowly. After his third boot, he felt right. On his next turn, he used Tug Watson's rocking step and met the ball with all his strength. His timing was perfect. As he left the ground with his follow-through, he knew this one was going places! A tremendous roar from the crowd paid tribute to the long, twisting boot. Inside, Chip was like a coiled spring. He'd show the Rock . . . when he got in there.

Three figures in black and white walked to the middle of the field, and the referee's whistle sent both teams to their benches. Soapy Smith led the way back to the bench and headed for the last seat. Someone else was already seated there, but not for long.

"I sat here all last year," Soapy yelled. "Look, you can see my rump marks. It's *my* seat! You wanna see the splinters?"

"I don't see your name!"

"Knock it off!" growled Thomas.

Soapy won the argument by sitting down on the inside and shoving his competitor off the end of the bench. Chip sat down next to Soapy and pulled a big VF towel over his shoulders.

"All right, Hilton, wake up!" Coach Rockwell called out impatiently. "C'mon, c'mon. You're out there with Morris for the toss. On your toes! On your toes!"

Chip sprang to his feet. "Sorry, Coach."

TOUCHDOWN PASS

"All right, now, Chip. If you win the toss—now remember—we want to defend the north goal. Let's get the benefit of the wind while we can; it might die down."

Out on the field Chip and Speed shook hands with Curt Warner, the big Hampton fullback and captain.

"Oh, co-captains!" smiled the referee. "Ready for the toss, now? All right; visiting captain's choice."

He turned to Warner and tossed a coin in the air. "Your call, Warner," he said.

Warner waited until the spinning coin reached its full height and then called, "Heads!" Heads it was. "We'll defend the north goal," he said.

Speed looked at Chip. "We'd better receive," Speed whispered. "You're the only one who could kick into *that* wind!"

"We'll receive," said Chip and headed for the bench.

"Plunk!" The ball sailed high and far down the center of the field to the ten-yard line and into the waiting arms of Badger. He started up the field fast but was dropped hard by Hampton's left tackle on the Valley Falls twenty-yard line.

The Big Reds came out of the huddle on the run.

"Ready, set, 1."

Collins faked to Williams and shoved the ball into Badger's stomach as Chris hit the line at top speed. For a second it looked as if he might break through Hampton's seven-man line, but only for a second. A swarm of tacklers met him a yard over the line and buried him. Collins tried Speed on a quick-opening thrust over Biggie Cohen, but he could gain only a yard. Biggie carried his Hampton opponent off the line a full five yards, but the orange and black defense met Speed right in the hole and slapped him down. Morris was a marked man. He'd been hit hard by every team Valley Falls met. He was hit again on third down for no gain.

Fourth down, eight yards to go with the ball on the Big Reds' twenty-two-yard line. Chip edged forward on the bench and watched the huddle. He remembered Coach had often said to kick in a third-down situation like that: the wind was bad, weak field position. A quick kick might have done it, but Badger needed to have more time with his kicks.

Now, better let Speed kick it from punt formation. Maybe Speed would try Tug Watson's end-over-end kick; the ball would stay low, and it might get Valley Falls out of this hole.

He breathed a sigh of relief when the Big Reds broke out of the huddle into punt formation with Speed back. Hampton went into a seven-man line and a diamond secondary, counting on a high kick into the wind. Chip's eyes shifted upfield. The safety man was standing on the Valley Falls forty-five-yard line. "Smart," he breathed. "He's counting on the wind."

The ball spiraled back to Speed, and he angled a low end-over-end kick, a Tug Watson kick, that barely cleared the line of scrimmage. Thirty yards up the field, the ball kicked up a little puff of dust and shot off, bouncing end over end. It seemed to pick up speed as it headed past the middle of the field and toward the northwest sideline.

The Hampton safety man had come in too fast, and he'd misjudged the speed of the bounding ball. Now, he was chasing it madly up the field. Right on his heels was Biggie Cohen. The ball dribbled out of bounds on Hampton's eighteen-yard line, and the Big Red boosters unleashed a thankful roar. Speed's kick had traveled sixty yards! Hampton's ball, first and ten.

Chip breathed a sigh of relief and moved back on the bench. But the next play brought him right to the edge of the bench again. Hampton retaliated with a well-disguised quick kick.

It worked. Speed was asleep. The ball flew over his head and right down to the five-yard line where it was grounded and held by the Hampton left end. Valley Falls started play deep in its own territory.

Valley Falls could not gain, and again it was fourth down as Morris went into kick formation. This time the Hampton players were ready. They shifted into a 7-2-2 defense formation.

Speed again used an end-over-end kick but drove it down the center of the field, barely clearing the charging Hampton line. The ball hit twenty-five yards away and bounced along the center of the field toward the converging Hampton backs. Again, Biggie Cohen was right behind the ball.

The nearest Hampton back approached the ball gingerly, playing it safe. His caution got him into trouble. The ball suddenly bounced sideways and struck him on the leg. He made a frantic grab for the careening ball but never reached it. Two hundred and fifteen pounds of concentrated fury struck him and sent him flying. Before the surprised boy hit the ground, a grim Biggie Cohen had gathered in the tricky ball. Valley Falls's ball, first down on Hampton's forty-five-yard line.

Cody sent Badger over left guard on a cross buck and a gain of two yards. Speed cut out to his right on a man-in-motion play with Cody carrying the ball on an in-and-out play to the right flank. The interference melted, and Cody was smacked down, hard, for a five-yard loss. This drive was going the wrong way.

COACH ON THE FIELD

Chip was muttering aloud now, "Kick it! *Kick it!*"

The Big Reds took a long time in the huddle, and Chip moved a little farther out on the bench. Then Cody did it! He took the ball from center, faked to Badger, and then ran out toward the right sideline. He was chased viciously by the Hampton center, who forced him to fade even farther behind the line of scrimmage. Cody turned in desperation and threw the ball laterally across the field to Ted Williams.

Chip saw it coming and so did everyone else. Hampton's defensive back caught the ball on the dead run and sprinted to the Valley Falls three-yard line before Speed hauled him down. Hampton came out of its huddle quickly, and Martin, Hampton's powerful running back, drove through the middle of the line. A deafening chant rose from the Valley Falls rooting section.

"Hold that line! Hold that line! *Hold that line!*"

No use looking at that piled-up mass of players. Chip's eyes searched for the figure in the striped shirt. The official had followed Martin into the line. This was going to be close.

Chip's heart sank as the linesman emerged from the pile of figures and threw both arms high in the air. Hampton had scored! The place-kicker dashed into the game from the Hampton bench and successfully kicked the point after touchdown as the quarter ended. Score: Hampton 7, Valley Falls 0.

Speed elected to receive as the teams changed goals. Hampton kicked to Williams, who was dropped in his tracks on his twenty-five-yard line.

It was the Big Reds' chance now. With the wind at their backs, now was the time to get some points. Speed broke through the line for six yards. Badger hit for two.

Cody tried a quarterback sneak but was inches short of a first down. Speed called, "Time out!"

Chip's heart jumped. "Report for Badger, Hilton."

"YEA—BADGER—RAH! RAH—RAH—HILTON!"

Chip lifted his knees high and swung his arms as he ran toward the referee. A moment later, he joined Speed who stood twelve yards back of the ball, talking to Collins.

"Chris could have done it!" Cody said obstinately.

"Too dangerous—better kick," warned Speed.

Chip interrupted. "What's too dangerous?"

"Running the ball," explained Speed.

"Heck, yes!" agreed Chip. "It's fourth down, and we're on our own thirty-four."

"Time, boys," the referee called.

Cody was down on one knee in the huddle. "Kick formation, Speed back, play thirty-two on the count of—"

"Signals off," said Speed. "It's too dangerous, Cody."

"I'm callin' the plays." Cody was belligerent. "Same play, count of three."

They broke from the huddle and went into kick formation. Thirty-two was a straight, hard drive through the center of the line on a direct shot to Chip. Speed, back in the kicking position, was adjusting his feet and holding out his hands, faking for all he was worth.

"Ready, set."

The pass from center was low and to the left, but Chip's big hands closed over the ball. He chugged his cleats desperately and sent his 180 pounds virtually right up Ted Williams's back. Williams stopped suddenly as if hit by a truck. Chip whirled to his right and surged forward but was met by the whole left side of the Hampton line. He knew he would need every inch, and, even as he fell, he tried to drive ahead.

The referee pushed into the pile of players. He knew it was going to be close too. It was close—a measuring play. A stilled crowd watched the linesman and his assistants run onto the field with the measuring chain. A deafening roar greeted the referee's signal of a first down. Cody's gamble had worked. Chip smiled grimly.

A minute later it was fourth down again and five long yards to go. The Big Red offense just couldn't get started. Chip kicked a long, high punt. The wind caught the ball and carried it over the goal line for a touchback. The rest of the half was a kicking duel. Chip's booming punts gradually forced Hampton back, but time ran out. Score at the half: Hampton 7, Valley Falls 0.

When the second half began, Chip was again on the bench. Coach Rockwell had ignored him completely during the intermission. Speed had the choice at the beginning of the second half and elected to defend the north goal. Hampton received and in just nine short plays marched the length of the field to score again. The kick after was wide. Hampton 13, Valley Falls 0.

A stunned opening-game crowd sat silently as Hampton continued to dominate the game. Just before the end of the third quarter, however, Speed brought the discouraged home fans to their feet when he intercepted a Hampton pass on his own ten-yard line and ran it back ninety yards for a touchdown. The crowd went wild! Hampton 13, Valley Falls 6.

Coach Rockwell grabbed Chip by the shoulders. "All right, Chip! You can do it! Get us one more! Report for Badger."

Chip dashed across the field, straightening his helmet as he ran. His thoughts raced ahead of his purposeful strides as he headed for the huddle. He'd kick that ball clear out of the stadium.

"Signals!" Cody called. "Kick formation, play thirty-one, on the count of—"

"Check signals," exclaimed Chip.

"I'm running this team," spat Cody. "The play has been called. Count of two."

Chip grabbed Collins by the arm. "Hold it, Cody. Coach said to kick it."

"Oh, yeah?" snarled Collins. "Leggo my arm. Quarterback calls the plays. Coach told all of you guys that! Thirty-one's the play, quarterback sneak, count of two."

"Yeah, Cody," drawled Badger sarcastically, "but it's nice to have a coach on the field. You don't seem to realize who you're talkin' to."

Chip drew a deep breath and glared uncertainly at Badger. Then he remembered the possibility of a penalty for too much time in the huddle.

On Cody's "hup," the Big Reds went up to the line. Their steps were slow and uncertain. They didn't like this. Biggie Cohen blew his breath out through gritted teeth.

"Ready, set."

Collins followed Trullo desperately, but he and the center were met at the line of scrimmage and smashed to the ground under a pile of bodies. The Hampton line never gave an inch. The score remained Hampton 13, Valley Falls 6.

Anger began to burn slowly in Chip. He'd had just about enough of this . . . taken about all he could.

COACH ON THE FIELD

Just then, Jordan Taylor, Soapy Smith, and Chris Badger went in for Collins, Trullo, and Hilton.

Coach Rockwell was furious. "I thought I told you to *kick!*" he raged at Chip. "What's the matter? Lose your nerve?"

Chip sat down on the bench without a word. Well, it was Rock's own fault. He'd said the quarterback ran the team on the field. No one—not even the captain—was to challenge the quarterback's selection of plays.

Without thinking, Chip raised his helmet high in the air and smashed it to the ground with all his strength. A minute later the quarter ended. Now it *would* be bad . . . last quarter . . . and against the wind.

That one little point after touchdown was getting bigger and bigger. He should have *made* Cody Collins listen and kicked that extra point at all costs.

Hampton and the wind kept the Valley Falls running attack completely bottled up. Rockwell sent Collins back into the game, but Speed couldn't match Hampton's kicking, and the Big Reds were gradually forced back to the shadow of their own goal.

Chip knew he could have matched Hampton's kicking even against the wind, but he also knew Coach Rockwell had pinned the responsibility on him for the extra point Valley Falls hadn't scored. Now Chip was paying for it.

He leaned forward and gripped the bench. Maybe the Big Reds would be lucky. Speed might break away.

The only support from the Valley Falls stands now was a flat, discouraged "Hold that line, hold that line." The Big Reds held but only because of the fighting, defensive play of Biggie Cohen, Ted Williams, Speed, and Soapy Smith. Soapy broke through Hampton's line three times in a row to stop Curt Warner cold. He was in on every play.

Trullo might be a better offensive player, Chip reflected, but he couldn't match Soapy's intensity on the defense. That's what this game was now, as far as Valley Falls was concerned, all defense. The Big Reds hadn't made a first down in the second half.

Chip looked at the scoreboard clock in despair. Only three minutes left to play, Big Reds' ball, second down and eight yards to go. Cody called Speed's number. Morris tried to get around the left end but was smeared for a nine-yard loss. Third down now, seventeen yards to go. The ball was on the eleven-yard line. Valley Falls came out of the huddle slowly and went into a kick formation, with Speed back.

Soapy's snap was wild, nearly over Speed's head, but he caught it. There was nothing for him to do except run. He had scarcely taken three steps before a swarm of Hampton linemen snowed him under on the three-yard line. It was fourth down now, twenty-five yards to go.

Chip groaned and buried his head in his hands. A second later he was yanked to his feet. "All right, Hilton," hissed Coach Rockwell, "get in there for Badger and kick that ball. Let's see if you have enough guts to kick us out of *this* hole!"

Chip grabbed his helmet and forcefully fastened the chin strap. He'd kick the ball all right . . . if he had the chance, but it was a little late for a kick after you were whipped! Valley Falls was down seven points with less than three minutes to play!

As he flashed out onto the field, he glanced again at the clock. Speed had called for a timeout and was standing near the goal line, talking to Biggie Cohen. The Big

COACH ON THE FIELD

Reds were down—mentally and physically. They needed a break. Ted Williams and Soapy Smith were standing beside the ball, hands on hips, silently glaring at the big scoreboard at the north end of Ohlsen Stadium. Those not bent over with hands on knees were resting with one knee on the ground. They were a defeated group.

Chip reported to the referee then joined Speed and Biggie. He slapped Speed on his shoulder pads and pointed to the clock. "Come on, you guys," he said, "there's still time!"

"Two minutes! Are you nuts?" Speed was disgusted. "The way we're backin' up, we'll score for Hampton in another minute."

"No, we won't. Listen . . ."

Speed listened and then shook his head. "It's dangerous, Chip. Too dangerous!"

"What have we got to lose?" gritted Biggie. "Do it!"

Chip's heart was pounding as he gripped Speed's shoulder in the huddle. Directly across from him, Biggie Cohen's black eyes were fixed on his face. Biggie nodded his head and shook a clenched fist in his direction. Chip scarcely heard Cody's "Punt formation, Hilton back; kick on the count of three."

As they left the huddle, Chip nearly tore Soapy's head off as he caught him by his face mask. "You give me a *good* pass Soapy, or else!"

Chip was standing in the end zone, one yard short of the end line. Soapy's long snap was perfect. Chip faked the kick and dodged to his right. He barely missed stepping on the end line as he evaded Hampton's charging left end. Then he cut loose at full speed to his right, running just inside the sideline. It seemed as if the whole Hampton line was bearing down on him—had him surrounded.

TOUCHDOWN PASS

Thirty yards up the west sideline, Speed was running for dear life—all alone. Chip danced back another step, cocked his arm, aimed the ball for the fifty-yard marker, and let it fly. The ball didn't reach the target, but it did reach the eager, outstretched hands of a racing Speed Morris who never broke stride as he caught the ball and raced toward the Hampton goal line. Touchdown pass! Score: Hampton 13, Valley Falls 12.

Euphoria broke loose on the field, and the crowd was in seventh heaven in the stands! Chip was mobbed by his cheering teammates. On the sideline, in front of the Valley Falls bench, Coach Henry Rockwell stood with his hands on his hips. This was the Rock's fighting pose. His jaw was hard, and the cords of his neck bulged. His eyes were blazing with anger. This didn't look like the face of a coach of a team that had just scored!

The only person on the wildly celebrating bench to note Coach Rockwell's behavior was the one person who knew him best—Chet Stewart.

When Chip had faked the kick and had run to his right to set up the pass, Stewart had watched in amazement. Hilton had deliberately disobeyed Rock's orders and the quarterback's signal. That probably meant Hilton's suspension from the team and probably meant Speed Morris would be dropped too. One thing was sure—Hilton was in hot water again. This time, it was of his own doing.

Out on the field, the players were mauling Speed, pounding him on the back unmercifully, and slapping high-fives. The referee's warning whistle ended their celebration. This game was still lost. . . .

Speed, still gasping for breath, knelt seven yards back of the ball. Chip pointed to the exact location where Speed was to spot the ball. A murmur went through the crowd.

COACH ON THE FIELD

Soapy's snap from center was perfect, and Speed spotted the ball down on the mark. The toe of Chip's shoe drove through the ball. In an instant the ball split the posts and sailed into the jubilant crowd behind the end zone. Chip turned and looked at the scoreboard: Valley Falls 13, Hampton 13. Forty seconds to play!

Hampton received and ran the kickoff back to its thirty-yard line. Deflated, they threw four straight desperation passes, all of which landed incomplete. As the last pass was batted down, the gun went off and the game was over.

A nearly uncontrollable mob of cheering fans swarmed out on the field. Chip and Speed were slapped and hugged by happy fans. A tie score had seemed impossible—it was a moral victory.

Later, three coaches sat in the athletic office and listened to the happy players in the dressing room. Stewart was nervous. He had expected Coach Rockwell to drop Hilton from the squad right after the game.

"That was some pass," he ventured, watching Coach Rockwell nervously.

"Could've been lucky, you know," said Thomas doubtingly.

"It wasn't lucky," said Stewart. "That pass traveled fifty yards in the air, and any kid who can throw a clutch pass that far is OK in my book." He shifted searching eyes toward Coach Rockwell. But Rockwell said nothing. He was wrapped in deep thought, his dark eyes fixed steadily on space.

A sudden thought struck Stewart. "Say, we don't have a play like that, do we?"

Coach Rockwell turned slowly and cast a withering look at Stewart. "No," he said, "we don't!" He walked to the window and watched the hundreds of cars maneuvering and slowly forming departure lines in the parking lot back of the stadium. The room was quiet for a long minute.

"No," Rockwell said, turning back toward Stewart, "we don't have a play like that." He drew in his breath and let it out slowly. "But, we're going to have something else though. We're going to have a new quarterback come Monday afternoon."

Stewart, half believing, sprang to his feet. "You mean—"

"Yep," said Rockwell. "Chip Hilton!"

CHAPTER 7

T
Quarterback

"COACH ROCKWELL wants to see you, Chip." Pop Brown nodded up the stairs toward the athletic office.

Chip had been dreading those words all day. Coach Rockwell was a strict disciplinarian. There just wasn't anything Chip Hilton could do except admit he'd deliberately disobeyed one of the coach's rules. He might as well get it over with.

Rockwell was already dressed for practice and was leaning over a flat table studying the laminated offensive and defensive play cards. He motioned Chip to a chair.

"Well, Chip," he began, "what's up?"

Chip's eyes wandered along the pictures on the wall, then over to Coach Rockwell, and then back to the pictures. "Sorry, Coach," he apologized, "I just figured the play might work. Guess I was just a little upset."

TOUCHDOWN PASS

There was no eye-shifting now. Chip faced around, and his gray eyes were steady as they met Coach Rockwell's questioning gaze.

"Bench fever, maybe," offered Coach Rockwell, kindly.

"A little, Coach, but I—I like to play."

"I know and I like kids who like to play too. In fact, I'm particularly strong for a kid who calls a play he believes in."

Rockwell studied Chip searchingly and then abruptly declared, "You've played your first and last game at fullback, Hilton."

"You mean I'm through, Coach?"

"I mean you can forget about the fullback job. From now on, you're a quarterback!" Rockwell announced with finality.

"A—a quarterback!" Chip was bewildered. "Coach, I never called a play in my life!"

"What about last Saturday?"

"That was just something that happened to click. I'd never be able to do that again—"

"Probably not. But you can handle a ball, pass, kick, run, and you've got football brains. That, plus one vital addition, completes the picture for a T quarterback. That vital addition is the confidence of the team and of the coach. I believe you can earn your teammates' confidence. You already have mine."

He gestured toward the white play cards on the table and glanced at the wall clock. "You're elected, Hilton. It's 3:30 now. Suppose you study those plays for an hour and then dress for practice. You'll find pencils and paper there on the desk. Write all those plays down carefully. I'll drop down to the Sugar Bowl tonight about nine o'clock, and you and I will have a little coaching clinic all our own. OK?"

Chip swallowed hard. "Sure, Coach," he managed.

Rockwell paused at the door. "A good quarterback knows the plays better than the coach, Chipper!" His thin lips curled in a half smile.

That evening, just as the Sugar Bowl student crowd was thinning out, Rockwell entered the store and walked directly to the storeroom. Petey Jackson abruptly ended a conversation and followed Rockwell. The coach was someone special where Petey was concerned.

Chip and Speed had been studying but pushed their books aside when Rockwell opened the storeroom door. Petey was right behind him but was quickly disappointed; Rockwell firmly closed the door almost in his face.

"Well," Petey managed, "that must be what they mean by conducting a secret practice."

Both boys were on their feet as the coach closed the door.

"How's the schoolwork coming along, boys?" queried Rockwell.

"Fine, Coach. We're both just about finished. See ya later, Chip," Morris said as he started to leave, but Rockwell stopped him.

"You stay, too, Speed. A little football quizzing won't hurt you, will it?"

"No, sir, Coach. Guess I can use it, all right." Speed's quick grin spread to his eyes.

"Now, Chip," Rockwell began, "I want you to sit down there at the desk and outline every play we have. Put each series on a separate page, and when you finish a play, you can explain it. Start with the line plays."

Chip first drew the play he knew best—about the only one Collins had ever called him for—a cross buck. He explained the play quickly. Two running backs charge diagonally into the line at opposite angles so their paths cross. The quarterback fakes a handoff to the halfback and gives the ball to the fullback who carries the ball over right guard.

Then, one by one, he outlined the rest of the line series, calling each play and the starting signal just as in a game. Coach Rockwell was pleased.

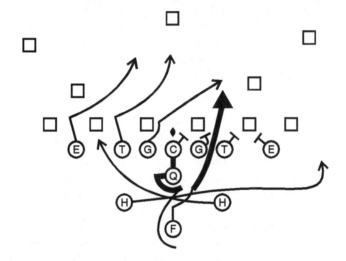

"Now, for a starter, let's throw a pass to Speed, in motion, out in the right flat." Coach Rockwell smiled, "You connected with him all right Saturday on the field, so you ought to be able to do it on paper."

Chip drew his conception of the play, starring Speed's approximate in-motion position when the ball would be snapped by the center, and showing the path of the pass by a dotted line.

"What's your footwork on that play, Chip?"

T QUARTERBACK

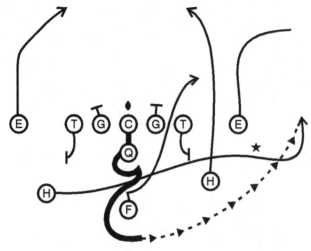

Coach Rockwell drew Chip out in the middle of the storeroom floor. "Show me how you fake your handoffs to the right halfback and the fullback before you run back to pass to Speed. Here, use my hat for the ball."

Chip gingerly took Coach Rockwell's new hat and bent over in the quarterback's position. Then he pretended to receive the ball from center, half-pivoted to the left so that his back was to the line, and held the hat completely concealed in the pocket made by his arms and stomach.

Holding the hat with his left hand, he faked out with his right as if to feed the right halfback and then continued his pivot. Transferring the hat to his right hand and extending his left, he faked giving the ball to the fullback. Then he covered the hat with both hands and, still facing away from the line, took three quick strides directly back.

TOUCHDOWN PASS

On the last step, Chip jabbed his right foot down hard on the floor and lifted the hat in his right hand as if to pass to his right.

"That's not bad, Chip." Coach Rockwell nodded his head, pleased. "You faked those handoffs nicely, and you kept the ball—the hat—well-concealed. But you made one little mistake that's important; you forgot to keep your head turned so you could see your receiver and the defense."

In the hour that followed, Chip and Speed received a thorough drilling in the T-formation plays. Coach Rockwell finally and grudgingly prepared to leave. Picking up his badly rumpled hat, he sheepishly tried to reshape it.

"Gonna be tough explaining what happened to this," he admitted, holding the hat in both hands and surveying it ruefully. "The boss, Mrs. Rockwell that is, bought it for me when school started. The only way I'll get a new one now is to win the sectional."

"How about the state championship?" Chip quizzed.

"I'd need a nice new one then, for sure." Rockwell laughed. "This one would certainly be too small!"

As Rockwell passed the fountain on his way out, Petey Jackson's eyes bulged. A sadly battered hat was drawn rakishly over Coach Rockwell's right eye, and a pleased smile highlighted his face. He seemed to strut a bit too.

In the week that followed, Chip alternated at quarterback with Cody Collins and Jordan "Air" Taylor. On the defense, Coach Rockwell used him at left half in the 6-2-2-1. Occasionally, when it was fourth down and big yardage assured a punt by the second string, the defense was shifted to a 6-2-1-2. Then Chip and Speed shared the two safety positions.

Coach Rockwell had already worked up several criss-cross plays for the two "Touchdown Twins," as the fans were beginning to call them, and Chip and Speed had created a play of their own. It called for a lateral whenever the ball was kicked to Chip down his side of the field.

Chip demonstrated good judgment in his quarter-backing. He selected his plays well and quickly proved he had become adept in his duties. At first, he had been clumsy in the pivoting and sleight-of-hand manipulation of the ball, but each day showed improvement.

However, Chip's progress seemed to work in reverse for the rest of the team. Something was wrong. Something had been wrong all week. In the scrimmages, nothing seemed to click. With the exception of Biggie Cohen, the line was slow, and the blockers lacked snap. When Trullo was at center, his passes to Chip were bad, his timing worse.

In the backfield, Badger was clearly antagonistic. He seemed to lose all his drive when Chip called the plays. Then, too, there had been Touchdown Twins jokes all week in the dressing room and on the field. Chip and Speed had not minded the good-natured digs of their friends, but the sly and sarcastic slams from Badger, Collins, and Trullo had begun to sting.

Before the week was over, Chip Hilton wished he had never heard of the Touchdown Twins. The jealousy and bitterness smoldering among the players, if allowed to continue, could ruin the chances of a team that only a week ago had displayed glimmers of championship possibilities.

CHAPTER 8

One-Man Show

THE BIG RED squad that assembled in the gym before the Weston game was lifeless. The players were slumped down, eyes downcast—almost sullen and indifferent. The rebellious undercurrent was obvious. Rockwell's worried brow and the long faces of his two assistants highlighted the coaching staff's awareness of the squad attitude. Even Pop seemed to have lost his spirit and drive.

Rockwell's eyes wandered along the line of faces, and without thinking, he began to pick out the strong ones. There were Hilton, Morris, Cohen, Williams, and Smith in one close row and, almost opposite, Badger, Trullo, and Collins. "That's it," he said half aloud, "that's it." He had worked this squad hard, too hard, maybe.

Too hard to notice it was a squad divided. Well, if he could just get by today's game, he'd do something about that.

ONE-MAN SHOW

Coach Rockwell started Chip at quarterback and kept him there the whole game. As the squad left the gym, Chip dropped back to wait for Collins.

"I'm sorry about the quarterback job, Cody," he said. "Guess we'll both see plenty of action though."

"Get lost, Hilton!" Cody clipped, barely glancing at Chip. "The Rock wants a two-man team—well, go ahead. See how far it gets you!"

The game was a nightmare. Nick Trullo's center snaps to Chip were designedly bad. Sometimes Trullo waited a split second after the signal to pass the ball; sometimes he snapped the ball before the signal.

Chip fumbled twice: once when Trullo hurried the pass and once when Nick held onto the ball after the snap signal. That time, Chip yanked the ball away from the ill-tempered center *too* hard, and the slippery pigskin dribbled back along the ground seven yards before he could fall on it.

Badger started slow and lacked drive. At no time did he smash through the line with his usual dash and power.

Weston was all set for Chip's passes to Speed. Someone had done a great job of scouting the passing combination; the speedster was covered at every turn. In desperation, Chip shifted his passes to the ends, Zach Harris and Miguel "Mike" Rodriguez, but neither was tall enough nor fast enough. He managed to hit Ted Williams with a buttonhook late in the second half, but the ball was soon lost on downs.

Neither team scored in the first three quarters. Then Weston caught fire and, starting on its own twenty-five-yard line, put on a sustained drive to carry the ball to the Valley Falls thirty-yard line. There Chris Badger failed to get up after a tackle, and Rockwell sent Cody Collins to replace him. Chip moved to the outside linebacker slot. Soapy Smith replaced Trullo on the defensive line. Chip was burning with rage—Badger wasn't hurt.

Collins kneeled down in the defensive huddle but was yanked to his feet by a raging Hilton. "I'll call the defense and the plays, Cody," he hissed. "Now the rest of you guys listen—"

Chip's words were bitter and personal. A slow anger began to rouse the fatigued players. Cody looked around the circle of players and was surprised to see the expressions on their tired faces were as unbelieving as his own. This was a new Chip Hilton!

Back to the defense they went—but in a different mood. Chip's words had hit home; they were fired up.

Weston started its line attack again, but the momentum had changed. Chip had whipped the whole line to a fighting pitch. It was a different team that dug in and charged through the Weston line in the last few minutes of the game. Speed lifted an incredulous eyebrow toward Biggie—neither had ever seen Chip like this.

Chip ranged along the defensive line, his gray eyes blazing. He was in every play, backing up the line with hard-hitting tackles. The Big Reds took the ball on downs but couldn't gain. Then Chip angled a high spiral kick to the center of the field. The Weston safety signaled for a fair catch but dropped the twisting spiral. Biggie Cohen and Soapy Smith chased the rolling ball to the Weston fifteen-yard line, where Biggie gathered it in.

After two running plays and a pass from Chip to Ted Williams missed by inches, Chip called for a field goal and with Speed holding the ball, split the posts with a perfect three-point placement. The game ended Valley Falls 3, Weston 0.

ONE-MAN SHOW

Late that night in bed, Chip couldn't sleep. With headphones on and in the darkness of his room, he reviewed the past week and the afternoon's game.

He knew something had to be done soon to develop some real team spirit, or the Big Reds were going to lose a lot of games. Well, he had fooled around long enough. The team had elected Speed and him co-captains, and that meant it was their responsibility to pull the team together. Long after midnight, Chip drifted off into a restless sleep.

A persistent ringing gradually forced its way into Chip's consciousness. His mind working slowly, he sat up in bed and listened. This was Sunday; he didn't have to get up early today. Church wasn't until ten o'clock. *Must have set the alarm clock without thinking.*

It was still dark, and he reached for the lamp. Just then the telephone rang again. He glanced at the clock— 2 A.M. Why, he'd been in bed only a couple of hours.

"Hello? Oh, hey, Biggie."

Biggie's voice was worried. "Sorry to wake you, Chip, but it's important."

"That's all right, Biggie. What's up?"

"My brother Abe was at the Academy tonight, and Mr. Browning and Joel Ohlsen had an argument."

"An argument! What about?"

"Fats was talkin' trash about you and Speed."

"What'd he say?"

"Said you and Speed hogged the ball, and you didn't care even if Valley Falls lost, just so long as you guys were the stars."

"How'd Mr. Browning get mixed up in it?"

"Mr. Browning said, nice-like, he knew you and Speed, and you weren't that kind. Said that wasn't true. Said Fats was wrong.

"Then Fats got mad and insulted Mr. Browning. Said no one was talking to him, anyway, and he'd better mind his own business.

"Abe was just about fed up enough to tell Fats off himself, when Mr. Browning left. Fats started asking all kinds of questions about who he was, where he came from, where he worked, and how he knew you and Speed. Said something about that 'wise guy' knowin' too much for his job and said he'd see if he couldn't do something about that."

"Thanks, Biggie. I'll look into it. You coming over tomorrow—er—today? Mom's expecting you for dinner after church. There'll just be you and Speed and Ted. We've got to do something about the team."

Chip worried the rest of the night. He knew how much the pottery job meant to Mr. Browning and his family. George Browning had suddenly become very important to Chip. He felt as though he had known him all his life. Mr. Browning was such a deserving person.

Chip was up early. His room faced the east, and the bright October sun gradually edged up and through his open window to warm his face and open his eyes. His mind was still on the problem that had kept him awake so long last night—the dissension on the team.

Downstairs, he headed straight for the porch and the Sunday paper. He turned to the sports page of the *Times* half fearfully. His fears were justified. The headline read:

VALLEY FALLS WINS DULL GAME
DEFEATS WESTON 3-0
Victory Is a One-Man Show

Chip dropped the paper and sat in silence. That story spelled more trouble. Now it would be "one-man show" all week. This was bad; something had to be done. He and Speed would have to figure out some way to pull the team together.

That afternoon, Speed, Biggie, and Ted Williams joined Mrs. Hilton and Chip for Sunday afternoon dinner. Afterward, everyone pitched in to do the dishes and had them put away in no time. Ted and Speed went out to the Hilton A. C. to shoot baskets while Chip and Biggie went into a private huddle in the living room to discuss Joel Ohlsen and George Browning. Chip expressed his fears that Fats might try to cause trouble for Mr. Browning. A short time later, Biggie and Chip joined the guys to shoot baskets.

"Look," said Chip, "the team's going nowhere fast. We've got to do something about it."

"Nowhere's right," agreed Biggie, "but fast! But what can we do?"

"I've got some ideas," said Chip. "This is what I have in mind. . . ."

Chip's plans were simple. He proposed, first, that he go see Badger, Trullo, and Collins that afternoon to try to patch up the bad feelings between the two groups. Second, he and Speed would drop by Coach Rockwell's house to see if they could get him to consider a few changes in positions: Ted Williams to left end where his height would make him a good pass receiver, besides strengthening that position offensively and defensively; Cody Collins to right half where his speed and blocking could be beneficial; Soapy Smith to left guard where his fight would bolster the middle-of-the-line defense; and Red Schwartz to right end where his basketball experience would mean another pass receiver.

Ted Williams was enthusiastic.

"Personally, I'd like a shot at end," he said. "I never played anywhere except on the line, and I think it would strengthen our defense. I'd be able to get out into the open quicker for passes too."

"Yeah," said Biggie. "Ted and I could work together and block to get Speed loose. Zach Harris just isn't big enough to block a tackle. That's why Speed hasn't been getting away."

"That would be a pretty solid team," agreed Speed, "but we wouldn't have any reserves to speak of."

Biggie laughed. "Who cares? If we stay in condition and injury-free, we won't need reserves. I read somewhere that Brown University once played a whole season with only eleven men—called them the eleven 'Iron Men.' If they could do it in college, then maybe we could do it in high school!"

"The Rock might go along with the team changes," Speed said thoughtfully, "but I don't think you'll ever swing Badger, Collins, and Trullo over, Chip. Besides, I think you're just looking for trouble going over on the South Side by yourself."

"Yeah, that's right," agreed Biggie. "You'll only put yourself in danger, Chip. You know how those South-Siders are—they chase guys from other parts of town just on principle." He studied his big, powerful hands a moment. "Guess I'd better go along," he added.

"We'll all go!" Williams said.

Chip laughed. "Then it *would* end up bad. They'd think for sure we were looking for trouble. No, I'll go alone. We'll meet at the Sugar Bowl at six o'clock. Speed, you call Coach and ask if we can see him tonight."

ONE-MAN SHOW

Chip rested his elbows on the top rail of the bridge leading to the South Side and pressed his chin against the cold, iron railing. He wore no hat, and the river breeze that swept through his close-cropped hair was cool and stimulating. He didn't have any idea what he would say to Chris Badger, Cody Collins, and Nick Trullo, but one thing was sure . . . Valley Falls High School wasn't going to go very far unless the animosity and jealousy were squelched.

Some time later, he proceeded across the bridge and turned up Riverview Avenue. His destination was the South Side drugstore. There a person could find almost any South-Sider at one time or another. Sure enough, the crowd of boys and young men hanging out in front of the store included Chris and Cody. They regarded Chip with hostile eyes. No one spoke. Chip placed both hands in his jeans pockets and spoke directly to Badger.

"Can I see you a couple of minutes, Chris?"

"You're lookin' right at me," Badger retorted coolly. "Help yourself."

"I mean privately."

"Sure! Why not? No skin off my nose," he quipped sarcastically.

Chip turned to Collins. "Want to get in on this, Cody?"

Collins clamped down on his chewing gum and regarded Chip steadily several seconds before answering.

"Yeah, maybe. Yeah—I guess so," he muttered.

The three athletes moved across the street and headed up the steps leading to the street above. Chip stopped at the first landing and leaned back against the railing. His eyes flickered once across the street toward the curious group; he took a deep breath, and then he plunged.

TOUCHDOWN PASS

An hour later, a discouraged and bitter Chip Hilton stopped again in the middle of the South Side bridge. The river breeze was cold and no longer stimulating. He stood there a long time, trying to figure out the reason for his failure to swing Chris and Cody around toward the idea of team unity.

Badger had been impassive; he'd said little. Collins had been scornfully antagonistic. Chip could understand the reactions of both.

Chris knew he had the fullback job cinched, now that Chip had been made quarterback. His attitude was due, chiefly, to his loyalty to Cody.

Cody realized Chip possessed certain abilities he could not match—kicking and passing—and he could see only riding the bench ahead, unless Chip got hurt. For Cody, the matter had ceased to be a competition for the quarterback position on the team. It had become a personal battle against Chip Hilton.

Only one rock had been thrown. One of a group of younger boys had hurled wide of his mark, and the rock had skipped ahead of Chip and bounced down the street. Chip had not turned nor had he quickened his pace. A shower of rocks would not have accelerated his deliberate withdrawal.

Chip was filled with cold fury and frustration. For one reckless second, he was gripped by a mad impulse to go back, to accept the thinly veiled challenge he had read in the eyes of Chris Badger and Cody Collins, to take them on—one at a time. Why wouldn't they even consider what he had to say?

Chip was conscious someone had said, "Lay off! Lay off!" but he didn't recognize the voice. He was past trying to recognize or realize anything except he had humbled himself only to meet scorn and ridicule.

Chip might not have been so discouraged if he could have heard Chris Badger explain why he had stopped the rock-throwing. Chip had struck the strongest possible chord in the stocky fullback's character that afternoon. It had been reflected in Badger's words: "I don't go much for Hilton and his crowd, but you've got to admit he's got guts! It took a lot of courage to come over here alone today—knowin' we'd all be here and knowin' the way we feel." He turned to Collins half apologetically.

"I know you hate the guy, Cody, but you gotta admire guts—guts and football ability. Chip Hilton's the best football player I ever saw!" His mouth twisted into an ironic smile. "This'll probably kill you, but, much as I dislike Chip Hilton, I voted for him for captain!"

CHAPTER 9

Eleven Iron Men

CHET STEWART and Bill Thomas exchanged glances and slipped quietly out of the athletic office. Coach Rockwell was completely oblivious to everything except the problem that gnawed at his mind and prompted the unfocused gaze of his eyes out the window, across Ohlsen Stadium, and far beyond the parking lot.

In the dressing room below, the loud voices of the squad carried up the locker room steps. This was the start of a new week—the start of the tough games too.

Red Schwartz, already dressed, was standing at the bulletin board studying the schedule. Chip joined him. Red shook his head grimly. "All tough, Chip. *All tough.*"

Chip cast a speculative eye over each of the remaining games. Yes, they were tough, all right, too tough.

Someone had scribbled the scores of the first two games on the card, and Chip eyed the remaining games

---

VALLEY FALLS HIGH SCHOOL
FOOTBALL SCHEDULE

Sept. 30	HAMPTON	Home	13-13
Oct. 7	WESTON	Home	3-0
Oct. 14	STRATFORD	Away	
Oct. 21	EDGEMONT	Home	
Oct. 28	SALEM	Away	
Nov. 4	WATERBURY	Away	
Nov. 11	DELFORD	Away	
Nov. 18		OPEN	
Nov. 25	RUTLEDGE	Home	
Dec. 2	STEELTOWN	Home	

---

with skepticism. Chip's thoughts as he stared at the bulletin board were interrupted by Coach Rockwell's voice: "Pop! Pop, can you hear me?"

"Yes, Coach, I hear you—"

"All right, send Badger, Collins, and Trullo up here."

As the three puzzled players headed up the stairs leading to Coach Rockwell's office, the curious eyes of every player in the dressing room followed their progress.

Red Schwartz voiced everyone's thoughts. "Wonder what *that's* all about?"

A half-hour later, the three boys joined the other players on the field. Their long faces and averted eyes discouraged questions. Coach Rockwell soon appeared and took charge of the practice. After a short time, he assembled the squad on the bleachers. Then he really poured it on. He discussed the past Saturday's game and each player's mistakes. He went right down the line, sparing no one. Even Biggie Cohen came in for a tongue-lashing.

Rockwell briskly walked up and down in front of the bleachers. When the Rock was angry, he paced like a caged lion. "I've had enough of this clique business," he growled. "From now on, you'll all pull together or turn in your uniforms.

"I'm making a few position changes too. Williams, you shift over to left end on the Red Team. Schwartz, you move out to right end. Cohen and Mazotta at the tackles; Smith and Leonard, guards; Trullo at center.

"In the backfield on the first squad, we'll line up with Badger at fullback, Morris and Collins on the wings—Hilton at quarterback. Now get out there and show me some teamwork."

That afternoon's practice and those that followed during the week proved Rockwell's lineup changes were working. The game at Stratford was a breeze—no contest. Chip and Speed elected to receive the first kickoff, and the Big Reds marched eighty yards on straight football to the Stratford three-yard line, where Chip called Chris Badger over right tackle. Badger bulled across the goal line behind Cody Collins for the score. Chip kicked the point after touchdown.

A few minutes later, Morris intercepted a Stratford pass and raced over for a second touchdown, and again Chip clicked on the extra point.

In the fourth quarter, Chip started a midfield passing attack that ended in a third touchdown when he pitched a fifteen-yard pass to Ted Williams standing all alone in the end zone. The successful conversion made it 21–0.

To top it off, Chip booted a perfect field goal from the twenty-five-yard line just before the game ended. The final score was Valley Falls 24, Stratford 0. After a big postgame dinner, the bus started the ninety-minute trip home. The happy squad sang, listened to music, and joked every single minute. Soapy Smith, as usual, had the best of several exchanges. Chip relaxed. He was dead tired. Coach Rockwell hadn't made a single substitution. At this rate Valley Falls would have its own eleven iron men . . . if they could survive.

It was just 8:30 when the bus pulled up in front of the Sugar Bowl, and everyone unloaded to collect Coach Rockwell's team-building treats of banana splits and pop. Coach Rockwell always permitted the boys a relief from football on Saturday nights. In fact, he encouraged the breather, provided it was not carried to excess.

A smiling and happy Petey Jackson greeted them. "Hi ya, guys. Nice going! Gimme five, Chipper! All right, now, how many splits?"

Chip joined Petey behind the fountain.

"Hey! What's that mean?" Red Schwartz pointed to a big cardboard poster pasted smack in the middle of the big mirror. "What d'ya mean, 'Petey Jackson's Sports Quiz'?"

Everyone stared at the cardboard.

A minute later, the Sugar Bowl was a cacophony of football questions and answers:

"Well, what d'ya know!"

"Look who's a sports expert!"

"What's the prize?"

"How you gonna prove those answers?"

Petey maintained a smiling calm, shrugging off all questions as he prepared the Sugar Bowl's elaborate banana splits—à la Jackson.

"I know the answers to the first two," Miguel said.

TOUCHDOWN PASS

PETEY JACKSON'S SPORTS QUIZ
WIN A PRIZE
A NEW QUIZ EVERY WEEK

1. What coach is known as the father of American football?
2. What president of the United States coached at two colleges?
3. Name the winning team, coach, and quarterback for Super Bowl I.
4. Who invented the huddle?
5. When were the first American football rules written?
6. What coach originated signals?
7. What coach invented the tackling dummy?
8. What player won, lost, then regained his Olympic gold medals?
9. What coach first placed numbers on his players' jerseys?
10. Who coached football against Catholic University in the afternoon and then coached his basketball team that night in Madison Square Garden?

"What crazy guy invented the tackling dummy?" Soapy demanded.

"Probably the same nut that invented the grass drill," said Red Schwartz.

"Bet his name was Thomas," volunteered Soapy, rolling his eyes.

"Gimme a pencil, somebody."

"Who ya kiddin'? Bet even Rock couldn't answer more than two or three of those questions."

"I can try, can't I?"

Down the street, toward the flats, the Saturday evening business at the Academy Bowling Center was in full swing. Tonight, Mike Sorelli was filled with mixed emotions. His hard mouth relaxed with a little smile every time he heard the bang of a cue on the floor and a triumphant, "That's it!" But his face clouded when he glanced back toward the bar. That end of the poolroom was filled with several pottery workers who'd had too much to drink and were testing the limits of Sorelli's tolerance.

One fellow in particular annoyed Sorelli. Tom Bracken was a caster. He had been employed at the pottery about six months. That was long enough to become disliked by all but a few of the men in the casting department. Bracken was always shooting off his mouth and criticizing something about his job and his employer. After a few drinks, he usually became even more unbearable. Tonight he was bitterly denouncing the findings of that week's casters' court.

Each week a casters' court was held to determine whether defective ware was caused by a caster's poor workmanship or because of faulty molds or an improper clay mix. Individual casters were paid for their ware when it was made, but defective pieces discovered during inspection were deducted from future wages if the casters' court ruled that the fault was poor workmanship.

Bracken was aggressively insistent. "It's the mix, I tell you! When the mix is bad, they blame the casters so they won't have to pay us for our work."

"Well," someone said, "they can't blame the casting department for this week's losses. *All* the ware was bad."

"Yeah, and I'll bet there'll be more too," growled Bracken.

Abraham Cohen was quietly munching a sandwich and listening intently to the heated dispute.

"Just wait until Monday," someone said. "Wait until J. P. sees all that discolored ware."

"What causes those green spots?"

Bracken looked at the speaker scornfully. "Same thing that causes the bad color," he said sarcastically. "Something in the mix, of course!"

"Well, since you know so much, what could be wrong with the mix?"

"Lots of things. Old nails or iron in the mix would do it if the clay and mix weren't checked carefully."

"No, the screen would catch them before contaminating the ware—"

"Not if they were in the storage vat."

"Look, isn't that what the magnet is for? The magnet'll pick out any metals—"

"Wanna bet?"

"Sure!"

"All right, let's ask Cohen. How about it, Abe?"

Abraham Cohen quietly shook his head. "Leave me out of the argument. I'm just a caster."

"Yeah? What d'ya think I am?" demanded Bracken, belligerently. He moved in front of Abe, almost pinning him in the corner.

Cohen smiled and, moving carefully around Bracken, started for the door.

"Well?" demanded Bracken, following Cohen. "Well, go ahead! Answer! What d'ya think I am?"

"You've got me there, bud," Abe said quietly. "Good night, everybody." He stopped in the dim light just outside the poolroom door and glanced at his wristwatch. He stood there for several moments and then struck out for the Sugar Bowl.

Although Chip was tired, he couldn't get to sleep. Abe Cohen had told him all about the poolroom discussion and about the spoiled ware. All the mix from the big agitator had been bad. It meant the loss of thousands of dollars to the plant and the loss of considerable bonus money to the workers.

Chip worried about the possibility that George Browning would be held responsible. Abe had admitted it looked bad, especially since Marty Dewitt, the chief chemist, had been home sick when the mix had been prepared. The foreman of the mixing department usually got his directions from the chief chemist, who would establish the formula mix ratio for the quantity of each material.

However, in emergencies, the chief chemist sometimes gave the foreman of the mixing department the formula and full responsibility. Abe didn't know whether Dewitt had given George Browning the formula or not.

Then Chip remembered the poolroom incident involving Fats Ohlsen and Mr. Browning, but he dismissed the thought. Fats was mean and ill-tempered, but even *he* wouldn't go to that extreme to get even with someone. And, yet . . .

CHAPTER 10

Hole in the Fence

J. P. OHLSEN was angry. Striding from one piece of ware to another, he examined each one carefully. There was a puzzled look on his face. Marty Dewitt, bundled up and obviously sick, followed with George Browning.

Ohlsen turned to Gordon Pinder. "What do you think of it, Gordon?" he asked.

Pinder's eyes shifted unconsciously toward George Browning and then back to the table on which the ware rested. Every piece was flecked with green spots.

"Well, J. P.," he said slowly, "it could be any number of things. But one thing is certain! It's copper, bronze, or brass!"

"Right!" agreed Ohlsen. "We've been purchasing our clay from the same British mine for years, and we've been running samples through the lab kiln too. The clay we're getting now is no different. Right, Marty?"

Marty Dewitt nodded in agreement.

HOLE IN THE FENCE

The Valley Falls Pottery was a personalized enterprise. J. P. Ohlsen's contact with every department head and foreman was close. He kept on top of them at all times. That day was one that would be long remembered. J. P. was on the move every minute, visiting every shop and department, and firing questions at everyone he met.

That night at dinner he scarcely touched his food. Mrs. Ohlsen tried to draw him out, to get him to talk.

"Who would be so irresponsible?" she asked.

"That's what I'm worried about. We put a new man in the mixing department a month or so ago. Just about the time the number-two agitator was fired. This bad ware could result from an error on his part or the carelessness of one of his men."

"Who is he?"

"A man by the name of Browning. John Schroeder recommended him."

Joel had been listening intently to the conversation. Now he spoke for the first time. "I've heard about him, Dad. He hangs out in the poolroom."

"Poolroom? How do you know this, son?"

"Wheels said he'd seen him drinking in there a lot of times."

J. P. rose abruptly from the table and began striding back and forth behind his chair at the head of the table. Then he turned to leave the room. At the door leading to the hall, he paused and spoke sharply to Joel.

"I would think you could choose better friends than Sorelli's crowd."

Mrs. Ohlsen struck the table with an open palm. "I don't think that is fair. Every time Joel tries to help you, you find something wrong. If Joel likes the Ferris boy, I'm sure it shows a very democratic spirit."

TOUCHDOWN PASS

J. P. started to speak but changed his mind. With a deep sigh, he left the room.

Monday evenings were always quiet at the Sugar Bowl. It was nine o'clock, and there wasn't a customer in the place. Chip and Speed sat on the high soda fountain stools studying the quiz card carefully. Petey had placed the correct answers under each question. Petey was happy, though his freckled face and vacant grin failed to reveal the degree of satisfaction he had gained from his new project.

Biggie Cohen

OK 1. Walter Camp is known as the father of American football.

OK 2. Woodrow Wilson coached at Princeton and _____

X 3. The Cleveland Browns, Paul Brown.

X 4. George Halas.

X 5. ~~1901~~ 1880

OK 6. Walter Camp invented signals.

OK 7. Alonzo Stagg invented the tackling dummy.

OK 8. Jim Thorpe won, then lost his medals.

OK 9. Alonzo Stagg first numbered players.

X 10. ?? Coach Henry Rockwell! HA!

HOLE IN THE FENCE

"How many did Biggie get right?" Chip asked.

"Six."

Speed was doubtful. "Let's see his paper," he said.

The two friends checked out Biggie's answers carefully. Biggie had answered all but the third, fourth, fifth, and tenth questions correctly.

"How'd he know all those answers?" demanded Speed. "Hey! Is this for real?"

"Sure," said Petey. "You guys want to know what the winner gets this time?" Without waiting for a reply, he continued proudly, "A five-pound box of candy! Bet Biggie's best girl's gonna like that—"

"Girl!" Chip countered. "Biggie's never looked at a girl in his life!"

"I wouldn't be so sure about that, Chip," Speed chuckled.

Chip went back to studying the football quiz. "Who *was* on that first Super Bowl team, and who thought up the huddle?"

Petey smiled and bent down behind the fountain a moment to pick up the spoon he had dropped.

"That's easy," he said. "The Green Bay Packers were coached by Vince Lombardi, and their quarterback was Bart Starr. The huddle most likely was first used at Gallaudet College, a school devoted to deaf students. Seems the varsity had to hide their sign language signals from their defensive team members during scrimmages."

"When *were* the first American football rules written?" Speed demanded.

Petey was enjoying himself immensely. He tossed the long soda spoon in the air and caught it expertly. He grinned.

"The rules were written by Princeton, Rutgers, and Yale in 1873," he said sweetly.

"Yeah! Well, who coached college football in the afternoon and then college basketball that same night?"

"That sounds like something Rock could do," Speed chimed in.

Again a spoon fell. Petey retrieved it and again smiled, ever more sweetly.

"Biggie said that, too, Speed. Actually, it was Coach Clair Bee of Long Island University. I think the winner of that football game received an invitation to the Sugar Bowl."

Speed glowered at Petey belligerently. "How do we really know these are the right answers?" he demanded.

Petey smiled loftily. "You can win a box of candy yourself if you can prove one of the answers wrong."

"Hah! I'd like to know where you're getting all these old football facts," Speed grumbled. "Bet it's the Rock! Maybe Pop! You're too thickheaded to scoop out—pardon the pun—those questions and answers all alone."

Petey laughed happily. "Wouldn't you like to know!"

Speed gave the thin Sugar Bowl manager a withering look and followed Chip as he got up and headed for the storeroom.

A little later, Biggie and Abe Cohen arrived and the conversation immediately centered on the spoiled ware and Browning.

"You think Mr. Browning will lose his job, Abe?" Chip asked.

"Can't say, Chip. It's a pretty big loss. Can't see why anyone would intentionally want to spoil all that ware unless they had something against the pottery or Browning and wanted him gone. Nothing to be gained!"

HOLE IN THE FENCE

Then he added thoughtfully, "Yes, there's more involved than formulas and mixing."

Biggie was shifting the box of candy from one big hand to the other. "I'm worried about the next batch," he said. "It's due to come out of the kiln on Thursday."

Biggie had worked at the pottery during the summers for years. Occasionally, he managed to work a weekend shift. The money he earned this way was being carefully saved for his college fund.

"It *will* be too bad if that new batch turns out the same!" Abe said. "You know, I've got a hunch it's someone who's got a grudge against J. P. himself. Heck, there's lots of ways anyone could spoil that ware!"

"How could someone spoil the ware?" Speed asked.

Abe smiled. "Oh, there's lots of ways that could be done. Someone could sneak into the mixing room and toss a few pieces of copper or brass into an agitator. One little handful would spoil every bit of clay in the batch. The magnet won't pick up copper or brass. Not everyone knows that though."

"When would anybody get the chance to do that?" asked Chip.

"Probably at night," said Abe.

"What about the security?" asked Biggie. "Wouldn't they see anyone foolin' around the agitator?"

"Look, Biggie," Abe said patiently, "anyone could get into the pottery works at night. Don't forget, there's usually only two watchmen for the whole plant—one outside and one inside. Anyone who knew his way around the operations at all could avoid them easy."

"But how could they get in?" asked Chip.

Abe laughed. "Through the fence," he said. "Don't tell me you don't know about the *hole in the fence*."

"Well, I don't. But the thing to do would be to watch this hole. J. P. ought to know about that, anyway—"

"That's right," agreed Biggie.

"Maybe so," Abe admitted, "but you keep still about *that!* Every guy in the place would be down on you."

"The *real* guys wouldn't," Biggie said confidently.

"Who *are* the real guys?" asked Abe.

"You're one!" said Biggie.

"I've gone through the hole. Guess about everyone has at one time or another—for coffee, sandwiches, a break, or something."

"I never did."

"That hole is like the secret password of a lodge or something. The pottery crew would never forgive anyone who caused it to be closed up."

"Well, if it's against the rules—"

Abe held up a broad, work-hardened hand.

"Look, Biggie, J. P.'s very demanding, all right. But deep inside he's an understanding man, Biggie—a very understanding man! He understands how hard we all work, and we produce quality ware—at least until recently! That's the concern."

Time during football season usually flew by so swiftly that Chip Hilton never could account for it. Not so this year. The two weeks since the Stratford game had been the longest he could ever remember. Valley Falls had won a victory over Edgemont, 14–13, but it had been a mighty tight squeak. The Big Reds also had won over the Salem Sailors by two touchdowns, but Speed Morris had sat on the sidelines with a sprained ankle. So much for the eleven iron men. Both games, which at the beginning of the season had been put down as no-brainers, turned out to be tough ones to win. Neither victory had contributed greatly to the prestige of the Valley Falls team.

The one bright spot during the past two weeks had been Coach Rockwell's decision after the Edgemont game that the job of calling the defensive signals was to go to Chip. That meant he would call the defensive alignments and signals in the future as well as the offensive plays as Valley Falls quarterback.

One night after practice, Chip had hurried home to find a dejected Taps Browning sitting, as usual, on the front steps of the Hilton porch. Taps had not attended school that day; he had not, in fact, been out of the house all day long. Chip knew why. The evening before, Abe Cohen had brought Chip the bad news. The ware from the second agitator had come out just like the first—contaminated and useless. George Browning had been laid off.

Taps told Chip his mother was deeply hurt and bitterly discouraged. She had condemned her husband, but he had not tried to defend himself. Sitting there on the front steps, Taps confided more about Mr. Browning's past. A long layoff initially drained the Brownings' savings and put the family in debt. After they climbed back on their feet again, Mrs. Browning's year-long illness had plunged them back in debt. Deeply discouraged and feeling beaten, Mr. Browning then started drinking and subsequently lost two jobs before coming to Valley Falls, sober and determined to make a fresh start. Now, through no fault of his own, he was out of a job again!

Chip was surprised Mrs. Browning so readily believed the worst of her husband and that Taps seemed inclined to side with his mother against his father. Only Suzy seemed to still trust and have faith in her dad.

Later that night, Chip came home from the Sugar Bowl to find George Browning waiting for him in the shadow of the porch.

"This is goodbye, Chip. I didn't want to leave without seeing you. You've been a great friend. I hope someday I can show you how much I appreciate all your help."

Chip had tried to get Browning to stick it out for a few days more but without success. He told Chip about the meeting with J. P. Ohlsen—how J. P. had said there was nothing he could do except to lay him off until the matter had been thoroughly investigated.

"Guess it's just J. P.'s way of letting a man go," said Browning. "He told me he'd call me just as soon as it had been definitely established where the responsibility rested. Then he gave me my paycheck." The man's face was despairing.

"Someday, the truth will come out, Chip. But I can't wait for that. I'm through in this town now. I've got to go somewhere else and find another job. Mrs. Browning and Jacob have a right to feel the way they do, I guess. Suzy will get along fine, but I wish you'd keep an eye on Jacob, Chip. He thinks there's no one in the world like you. He'll need help. Mrs. Browning can take care of herself—she's had to do it before. Jacob is such a sensitive kid though."

Chip promised to keep an eye on Taps, and George Browning, after assuring Chip he would write and send money home, walked off the porch and down Beech Street.

The evening after the Salem game, a despondent Taps had come over to the Hilton house and told Chip his father had left home. Chip had not revealed he already knew about George Browning's departure. Taps had said his mother was heartbroken and worried but wouldn't listen to his talk of quitting school and going to work. She was going to try to get part-time work.

That night Chip, Speed, and Biggie remained in the storeroom until midnight to discuss plans for keeping watch on the agitator room at the pottery. By now, all three boys were convinced the baffling accidents occurring at the plant, which had cost Mr. Browning his job, were the result of sabotage. They realized that their plans called for a certain amount of risk, danger, and the loss of many hours of sleep during a crucial stretch of the football season. As the three boys stood on the sidewalk before the darkened store, they went into a quick huddle. They placed their right hands in a three-way clasp.

"We're in this together, guys," said Chip. "It looks as though there's a job to do—so let's see it through."

"We're with you, Chip," said Speed and Biggie in unison.

CHAPTER 11

The Hard Way

TUESDAY, OCTOBER 31, was only the first of many big days which were to occur in Chip Hilton's life, but so far it was probably the most important. It marked the first day he'd ever reached an important decision through his own reasoning and planning. He had resolved to see J. P. Ohlsen personally and hear directly what justification there had been for Mr. Browning's job loss.

One of Coach Rockwell's favorite sayings was: "Go the hard way! Whenever you find it easy to break through an opposing lineman—beware of a mouse trap!"

Well, Chip reflected, this was the hard way—right to the top person, so to speak.

He felt a little shaky when he thought about it. He was going straight to J. P. to question something that was none of his business . . . unless he could justify the act by virtue of sure knowledge of an injustice to a friend.

THE HARD WAY

Mary Hilton was surprised to find Chip dressed in a sport coat and tie waiting for her in the kitchen at 6:30 in the morning. "Why, Chip Hilton, what on earth got you up so early? Is there something special happening at school today?"

"Nothing much! I'll tell you about it later, Mom."

"It certainly must be important to get you up this early!"

Chip walked down Beech Street and then continued to Main Street, past the Academy, and through the flats to the pottery office.

Mrs. Carolyn Wenzel smiled brightly at Chip and then cast a surprised glance at the office clock. It was 7:45 A.M. Carolyn Wenzel had been J. P. Ohlsen's executive secretary for many years. She was very efficient, and people said she knew more about the pottery business than J. P. himself. She had known Chip's father well and had watched Chip grow up.

"You'll be Mr. Ohlsen's first order of business," she promised. "Come right in here and sit down in the outer office. He'll be along any minute now."

J. P. came briskly into the offices, walked directly into his private office, and sat in the chair behind the big mahogany desk. Mrs. Wenzel waited quietly until the big man had scanned the papers piled neatly on the desk, and then she glanced at Chip. He rose and stood there shifting his weight from one foot to the other.

"Chip Hilton is here to see you, Mr. Ohlsen. He's been here since 7:45."

"Oh, thanks, Carolyn. Come on over here, Chip. Sit down. What's on your mind so early this morning, son?"

Chip had rehearsed what he wanted to say, but his mouth was dry, and he was stuck for a place to start. He swallowed hard.

"I—I wanted to talk to you about Mr. Browning and the bad ware, Mr. Ohlsen," he managed.

"That's a pretty tough subject around here right now, Chip. What do you know about it?" J. P.'s voice was friendly, and Chip felt more at ease. Chip's father had greatly admired J. P. Ohlsen and had passed much of his liking along to Chip.

"Not much, sir, but I know Mr. Browning very well, and I know he wouldn't let anything happen to the ware."

"But something *did* happen, Chip."

"I know, sir, but it couldn't have been Mr. Browning's fault. The bad ware went through the mixing department before he was even hired, and besides, he'd have nothing to gain—"

"The mixing is only a small part of it, Chip. Browning was in charge of the mixing department two or three weeks before the clay went to the casting department.

"You see, Chip, there's more to this than an error in the formula or in the mixing or in the casting.

"Browning was a new man here; he was placed in an important position without real testing. He did have enough years of experience, specialized training, and acceptable references. However, he admitted to me personally and privately he had lost two previous positions because of certain weaknesses. I liked his honesty, his obvious sincerity. But the company has suffered a severe loss, and the men have lost considerable bonuses. The responsibility must rest somewhere. George Browning accepted the responsibility of the position—he must accept the responsibility of the results."

THE HARD WAY

J. P. Ohlsen looked deep into Chip Hilton's anxious gray eyes for a long second, and his stern face softened. Then he breathed deeply, rose from the leather-backed chair, and moved to the big window overlooking the plant.

His heart went out to this boy. He was a chip off the old block, all right—turn back the clock a few years and this teenager could have doubled perfectly for Big Chip Hilton. In spite of himself, he compared this fatherless boy with his own son. Joel's stories about Bill Hilton's boy didn't ring true. This kid had too much courage—too much loyalty—to stoop to unfair tactics.

He turned back to Chip. "Chip, you can be sure George Browning will receive every consideration. If you hear anything you think I should know, get in touch with me immediately—at any hour—day or night."

Right after lunch, Chip, Biggie, and Speed headed for the library. They sat at a table in a corner of the quiet reference room. Speed was still hobbling on his injured ankle, and Mr. Spence, the librarian, fixed eyes upon them with obvious annoyance.

Chip gingerly pushed a large globe along the table, and the three friends leaned their heads close together. Chip said nothing about his talk with J. P. Ohlsen. Biggie passed on the information that a new mix was going right back into the number-three agitator the following day. Abe and his father, Nathan Cohen, had worked out a plan so that number three could be constantly watched in two shifts.

Mr. Cohen's shop bench overlooked number three, and Abe's table in the casting department was right in line with the big agitator. They had worked out a schedule so it would never be out of sight of one of them from 7:00 A.M. to 4:00 P.M. Nathan Cohen's best friend, Bill Hartrampf, worked at the same bench the following shift. He could be trusted not to fail Mr. Cohen.

That left only the late shift, 11:00 P.M. to 7:00 A.M. to worry about.

"Only!" exclaimed Speed. "Who's gonna take that turn?"

They were startled by the sharp rapping of a ruler and whipped their heads around to meet Mr. Spence's angry glare. "Quiet! You boys keep quiet!" he hissed.

"We'll have to cover the third shift," whispered Chip firmly. "You and Biggie and me. That's *who!* We'll take turns!"

Speed was puzzled. "How we gonna get in?" he asked. "Where we gonna hide?"

"We'll work that out. We've got to! We'll use the hole!"

"What if we get caught?"

"We won't get caught!"

Chip waved an impatient hand that accidentally struck the big globe and sent it tumbling against the wall. Only a miraculous catch by Biggie saved them from disaster. Sheepishly, he righted the globe as Mr. Spence came scuttling down the aisle.

"That's enough! Leave the room and don't come back."

"You didn't have to turn the world upside down," quipped Speed as Chip closed the library door behind them.

Chip hurried through his supper that night and rushed down to the Sugar Bowl. Petey Jackson was leafing through a book and covertly writing on a large piece of paper when Chip passed the fountain. Petey flipped a letter to Chip. "Came this afternoon," he said, turning his attention back to his paper and pen.

THE HARD WAY

Chip sat down at the fountain and opened the envelope. The letter was from George Browning. He hadn't found a job yet but promised to write home and to Chip, too, just as soon as he got located. He again asked Chip to look after Jacob and Suzy. There was no return address. Chip looked at the postmark. The letter had been mailed from Maryville.

Petey was watching Chip expectantly. When the letter was tucked carefully away, Petey held out a large sheet of paper. "Some of this week's questions," he proudly explained. "See how many you can get," he challenged with a broad grin.

Chip studied the list carefully and then read aloud: "'What man organized, coached, captained, and played on the football teams of two colleges?'" He reflected a moment. "It'd have to be one of two men, I guess—Alonzo Stagg or Pop Warner. Right?"

Petey nodded. "Fifty-percent right! It was Stagg, but don't you tell anybody!"

"Don't worry," Chip reassured the exuberant sports fan. "Say, Petey! Chet Stewart's bringing some State game films down about nine o'clock. They use the T, and Chet wants me to see how their quarterback handles the ball. He's going to set 'em up in the storeroom. Mr. Schroeder said it was OK."

"Great!" Petey gasped. "Boy, I hope business is bad."

Business wasn't bad, but it wasn't to Petey's credit that it was good. He spent most of the thirty minutes it took Chet Stewart to run through the State film in the storeroom. Stewart reversed the tape again and again, stressing the technique State's quarterback used to conceal the ball from the opponents. It was clever, hidden-ball stuff, and Chip mentally catalogued the sleight-of-hand maneuvers he could use with the Valley Falls T-formation plays.

He shook his head admiringly. "State's quarterbacks sure can handle that ball!"

"You don't do so bad yourself, kid," said Stewart.

"Hope State asks Speed and me up again this year for their spring festival." Chip shook his head wistfully. "That was an experience!"

Chet Stewart placed a hand on Chip's shoulder. He was smiling a bit, but his voice was serious. "Look, Chipper," he said, "every big college in the country will be inviting you to look over their campus before you graduate from Valley Falls High. Most of the time, they throw the mold away when they make an All-American—but *this* time they didn't. Your dad was great, Chipper, but you're going to make him look like a substitute—and he'd love it!"

The strain had begun to tell on everyone at the pottery, from J. P. Ohlsen down to the three boys sharing the voluntary—but secret—watch over the mixer. It had not helped the team, which had appeared sluggish in practice.

On Tuesday, they had outlined the week's watches, and Chip had taken Wednesday night; Biggie, Thursday night; Speed, Friday. Chip's turn was to come again tonight. But so far nothing had happened. The week had slipped by uneventfully, and now here they were in Waterbury, in the visiting team's dressing room.

Chip was gripped by that pregame stress that always seemed to sap his strength and leave him with a pounding heart and a butterfly stomach. He dug his fingers into the wooden bench and held his breath.

"Schwartz and Williams at the ends, Cohen and Mazotta at the tackles, Smith and Leonard at the guards, Trullo at center—" Rockwell's eyes swept along the row of faces. "Taylor and Collins at the halves, Badger at full, and Hilton at quarter!"

Rockwell paced in front of the eager faces. The corded muscles of his jaw and the straight set of his tightly pressed lips were mute evidence of a strong emotion. His hands were clasped behind his back, and his black eyes snapped. He paused directly in front of Chip, and the words that tumbled one over the other were blurred by repressed anger and disappointment.

"I've never believed in rigid training rules; never wanted to say to a boy: 'If I catch you out after eleven o'clock, you're through.' Never felt I needed to say, 'Don't smoke!' or 'Don't do this and don't do that.' I've always believed the kids who made up the Valley Falls teams were interested in playing the game for the school and the team and because they loved the sport. Guess I've been wrong about certain players on this team. Disappointed too.

"We're a good team—undefeated! But that doesn't mean a thing unless the players on this squad have the right spirit. I hope I'm mistaken. That I'm misjudging some of you.

"But enough of that. This Waterbury team is tough. They're tied right now with Coreyville for the championship of Section One. I don't need to tell you what that means.

"You've already beaten the leader of Section Three— Edgemont. If you win today, you'll have to be considered one of the outstanding teams in the state. You'll have only three games to go, and I think you can win them all. Delford at Delford on Veterans Day; Rutledge, undefeated in Section Four, at home November 25; and Steeltown, defending champions of Section Two and of the state, at home on December 2. But this game today is the key game. We've got to get this one.

"I don't want to use Morris unless I have to. We'll need him at Delford, and I don't want to take chances with that ankle. You men can win this game, but you'll have to fight. Waterbury always points for us—they'll be up today. You'll have to play hard, and you'll have to play smart. All right, now. Let's go get it!"

As the Big Reds trotted out of the dressing room and toward the bleacher-terraced field, a great roar erupted. Chip was surprised, but the answer was quickly evident. Waterbury's blue-clad warriors were breaking out from under the south goal. When the Valley Falls forces ran onto the field, a faint cheer rose from the small crowd that had come with the team on this trip. The Waterbury stands added a slight courtesy applause.

Chip was tired. He had that worn-out feeling that comes only from an overworked sports brain or from too much mental strain because of an important personal problem. He was stale.

He breathed a weary sigh. This day would never end. Following the game this afternoon, he'd have to work at the Sugar Bowl until nearly midnight and then relieve Biggie at the pottery. Biggie was going to take over at eleven o'clock and wait for Chip to close up the store. The three-hour bus ride home would be a help though; he'd try to sleep. A good thing tomorrow was Sunday; he could sleep until 9:00 A.M. and then zonk out for a long afternoon nap after church.

Last Wednesday Chip had been concerned with the problem of explaining to his mother where he'd been the nights he had the watch. She never went to sleep until he got home from his work at the Sugar Bowl, and he didn't feel right about being away from the house and leaving her alone.

Mary Hilton knew something was troubling her son, but she was wise in the ways of handling Chip. She knew he would confide in her before too long. Her patience, as always, was rewarded. She had faith in her son.

Chip had sat silently at the supper table for a few minutes and then blurted out the whole story. Mary Hilton had studied Chip's worried face and skillfully drawn out all the details. Chip had told her about Abe and Mr. Cohen and Cal Bender, the night watchman the Cohens had taken into their confidence. Mary Hilton knew her son and understood how much he was wrapped up in this effort to help George Browning. Chip was growing up, she thought, and this was his idea. Every boy was entitled to a little leeway in the growing stage, and if Mr. Cohen and Cal Bender knew about the night watches, the boys would be in good hands. Young Morris was a bit flighty at times, but the Cohen boy was sound.

After he had broken the ice, Chip had given his mother all the details. She had been almost as enthusiastic about the plan as he had, Chip reflected. Not that he was so enthused now; he was too tired.

While these thoughts had been running through Chip's mind, he had been going through the usual pregame warm-up drills automatically. Even while he was sending his booming punts soaring high in the air, his thoughts were far from Waterbury.

In the morning mail delivered to the Sugar Bowl there had been another letter from George Browning. It contained good news. Mr. Browning had gotten a job in Steeltown. It wasn't nearly as good as the Valley Falls job, but at least it was a start. He was lonesome for his family in Valley Falls and gave Chip his address. He asked Chip not to tell anybody where he was or about the new job until he could get his family back on solid ground. He said not to worry about him, and he was regularly in touch with his family.

On the bus ride to Waterbury, Chip had tried to rest, but it was impossible. John Schroeder had given Petey Jackson the afternoon off, and Rockwell had let Petey ride over with the team. That was a mistake! Petey and Soapy had kept the bus in an uproar despite Coach Rockwell's quieting them down several times.

At frequent intervals, cars from Valley Falls containing Big Red fans had gone flying by, honking their horns, waving banners, shouting, cheering, and singing. Fats Ohlsen, completely ignoring the bus, had passed in his convertible, top down and stereo blasting. Chip had caught a glimpse of Wheels Ferris, another boy, and three girls in the crowded car.

The shrill blast of a whistle jarred Chip back to football, and he joined the circle around Rockwell in front of the bench. Rock motioned Chip and Speed toward the middle of the field where the Waterbury captain and three officials stood waiting. "Wind's from the south," Rock asserted. "Defend that goal if you win the toss or get the chance."

But they didn't have the chance. The Waterbury captain won the toss and elected to defend the south goal. Chip eyed Speed. "Kick it," murmured the stocky back.

"We'll kick," echoed Chip.

THE HARD WAY

Back in Valley Falls, Doc Jones and John Schroeder were huddled over a little radio in Doc's office above the drugstore. Not that they were any different from hundreds of other Valley Falls fans who had been unable to make the trip. Radios were blaring all over town, and they all were tuned to Waterbury's WBC station, which was hooked up with Valley Falls's own WTKO. This year's Big Reds had caught on; this might be *the* year.

Stan Gomez was right on the scene and was teaming with Waterbury's Casey Malone in reporting the game. Malone's excited voice had just announced the kickoff.

"The ball to the Waterbury five-yard line. What a start! This Hilton kid really can kick—Carlos Gonzalez took that kick for Waterbury. He's driving straight up the field. The Blues formed a wedge for the big boy—Wow! Number 77—who is that guy, Stan? Number 77 broke through that wall and spilled Gonzalez all over the field. He's still down. Cohen was the player who spilled him—Valley Falls's left tackle. Gonzalez's out, and the Blues are taking time-out too.

"Time-in again. Out of the huddle, up to the line. Waterbury is using the single-wing formation—there's the snap from center—Melvin Stevens has the ball. He's running wide to the right—that big kid with the number 77 on his back is in there again. He stripped the interference—Stevens is running all alone out there in the right flat now. Number 88, the Big Reds' left end, is chasing him back—there's the tackle. Stevens is down clear back on the ten-yard line near the east sideline. It was Williams who made that tackle. What a pair—that 77 and that 88—Biggie Cohen and Ted Williams!"

The radio in Mike Sorelli's was tuned to the game too. Even the men playing eight-ball called out their shots in subdued voices as the radio blared out the play-by-play action.

Casey Malone was calling the game when Waterbury had the ball, but Stan Gomez took over when Valley Falls was on offense. It was intermission now, and the two sportscasters were reviewing the first half.

"But I thought you said the Big Reds had a strong offense—"

"They have, Casey, normally, but don't forget Speed Morris is on the sidelines with a sprained ankle. You can't take a runner like him off anybody's team without slowing down their running attack."

"Well, you may have something there, Stan, but that Valley Falls attack had better get started soon, or we're going to see a big upset here this afternoon. Waterbury's pushing 'em all over the field. About the only thing saving the Big Reds so far is Hilton's kicking."

CHAPTER 12

The Flea-Flicker

THERE WAS a strange silence in the Valley Falls dressing room. Chet Stewart, Bill Thomas, and Pop were busy with their usual between-halves duties but occasionally glanced at one another with puzzled eyes. The players were bewildered too. Coach Rockwell had not followed them into the dressing room! This had never happened before. In fact, he was usually the first one in the door.

As the precious minutes flew by and Rockwell still did not appear, Speed and Biggie joined Chip and the three spoke in hushed voices.

"Wonder where he is," said Speed.

Biggie shook his head. "Maybe he's sore. We're not playing that badly—are we?"

"No," said Chip, "something's wrong! He'd be here if it wasn't something important. Hey! We gotta get some kind of an offense going, or we're licked. They're playing us just right. They know we don't have anyone who can go outside but you, Speed, and they're bunching up the line and concentrating on pass defense. We've got to spread 'em out, some way."

Speed jumped up and down on his injured ankle. "Look, Chip, I can play. My ankle's all right. Pop said I could run on it!"

"Why doesn't he put you in then?" Biggie challenged pointedly.

"You know why, Biggie," Chip waved a hand in an impatient gesture, "you know how Rock is about injuries—"

"But if Speed's all right—"

Chip interrupted. "You heard what he said. He doesn't want to use Speed until the Delford game."

"What's the use of thinking about the Delford game if we don't win this one?"

Chip was impatient. "Because Delford's in our section for one reason, and because we haven't lost this game yet—for another!" He felt a sudden surge of anger. It was the first time this game had gotten under his skin. His gray eyes narrowed, and he struck the palm of his left hand with a clenched right fist as the words clipped out of his mouth.

"Now listen! We'll try the flea-flicker from punt formation with the ends and the halfbacks out wide. Remember the play? We practiced it when we were freshmen. The play starts out like a double reverse with the ball coming back to the quarterback, who then throws a long pass. Then, the receiver laterals the ball to the trailing teammate. We gotta use a spread of some kind to open up that Waterbury line, and that's an easy one. Biggie, you explain it to the line—hurry!"

THE FLEA-FLICKER

"Speed, you explain it to Chris, Cody, and Jordan, and I'll check it with Schwartz and Williams. Get going! We gotta hurry!"

Upstairs in the Waterbury principal's office, a red-faced, angry Rockwell turned away from a downcast Joel Ohlsen and glared at the two police officers who were standing by the door.

"He's just a spoiled kid who has more money than he knows what to do with," Rockwell sighed bitterly, shaking his head. "He's no more a gambler than I am!"

"But he was waving a big roll of money, Coach, and attracting a lot of attention," said one of the officers quietly. "Our orders are to arrest all gamblers—"

"I'd think you could tell an arrogant school kid from a gambler!" Rockwell exploded. "Of course, it's wrong to bet on the games, but this kid isn't a criminal. He's just a show-off!"

The officer who had spoken looked at the man standing behind the desk. Waterbury Principal Madden nodded slightly. "Well, Coach," the officer said, "I guess if you'll take the responsibility—"

"I'll do that all right," Rockwell barked over his shoulder as he grasped the scared boy by the lapel of his brown leather coat.

"Now you listen to me, Ohlsen. If you get in my hair just once more, I'm going to have a talk with your father! Maybe I'll do it anyway!" He shoved the startled teenager out of his way, nodded curtly at the man behind the desk, looked contemptuously at the two policemen, and strode out the door. But it was too late. The teams were already on the field.

TOUCHDOWN PASS

Stewart and Thomas hurried to his side. "What happened, Coach? Is anything wrong?"

"Tell you later. All right, boys. Sorry I couldn't make the dressing room. Something personal. We'll start the same way we finished. You've got the choice, Chip. Defend the south goal!"

On the kickoff, Chip's foot met the ball exactly in the right spot, and the football sailed end over end above the Waterbury goal, beyond the end zone, and, after one bounce, into the stands for a touchback. It was a mighty impressive boot, and the stands paid him tribute. He had known the wind would do the work if he met the ball just right.

It was Waterbury's ball, first down, on its own twenty-yard line. As Chip trotted back to the safety position, he was muttering to himself, "If we can only hold them now and get that ball in time to try the spread before we have to go into the wind."

Chip had planned his strategy well. He meant to take advantage of the wind for the first eight minutes of the third quarter by kicking at every opportunity. He needed to keep Waterbury pinned back in its own territory, if possible. Then, when he got the ball, he'd try the spread and throw a couple of passes to set up the flea-flicker.

Keeping the ball in Waterbury territory, though, posed a problem. The Blues' running attack had been clicking; they had to be stopped. Chip decided to shift Badger to Jordan's position at defensive linebacker and to send Jordan back to his own safety position. Then he would take Badger's linebacker spot to ignite the line and make the team fight for yards.

But Waterbury had ideas of its own. The Blues made two quick first downs in succession, and Chip called time. The ball was on the Waterbury forty, first down and ten.

THE FLEA-FLICKER

In the huddle, Chip jumped on each lineman in turn. "You're named right," he said, glaring at Soapy. "They slipped through you like you were liquid soap! Hah!" His movements and facial expressions communicated disgust as he turned to face Lou Mazotta.

The serious-faced boy who played right tackle was one of the quietest guys on the squad. Mazotta was only five feet seven, but he packed 190 well-distributed pounds of fighting fury, once enraged. No one usually realized that he and his running mate, Robby Leonard, were around unless a special event brought them to someone's attention. Mazotta was short and powerful, but Leonard was tall and tied together with stringy muscles as strong as steel cables.

"Tackle!" Chip gritted, challenging Mazotta scornfully, "Hah, you don't know what it is to make a tackle. If you want to quit, quit on the bench!"

Mazotta's face flamed to a dark scarlet, but he said nothing. Chip knew he had *him* fired up, all right. Biggie Cohen, Ted Williams, Red Schwartz, Robby Leonard, and Nick Trullo all got a taste of Chip's tongue-lashing; he didn't quit even when time was called.

Waterbury started in right where it had left off—through the line. The confident Blues again tried their line attack. But this time, things were different. This time, seven angry, fighting, Big Reds linemen, goaded by their raging co-captain, stopped them cold.

On third down, Chip waved Jordan to the defensive back position, with Chris Badger, and fell back in the safety position himself. It was a good move, for Waterbury kicked, hoping to catch the Big Reds disorganized.

The ball bounced on the Valley Falls forty-yard line and twisted to the left, but Chip took the chance. He made a shoestring catch and was on his way up the west sideline. As he hit full stride, he heard Petey Jackson's shrill voice above the roar of the home crowd. Then all sounds were lost to consciousness as he drove for that midfield stripe. If he could only get over that fifty-yard line before the first tackler hit him, he would be in position to try the spread. It was now or never!

He flashed by the forty-five, crossed the fifty, and was down to the Waterbury forty-five-yard line before the first tackler hit him. Chip's long legs were driving now, and his momentum carried two more desperate Blues to the Waterbury forty before he was dragged down.

As Chip fought his way out of the pile of bodies, someone pounded a knee in his back, but he paid no attention. This was no time to be distracted, no time to lose his head.

In the huddle he called for the spread. "This is it, guys! On the second 'hup,' spread wide and stay onside. No need to charge now, just give me enough time so I can hit Schwartz or Williams with a couple of short passes. Cody, you delay a count of two and then run right toward Trullo—maybe we can connect for a short one. All I want to do is complete one or two short passes, and then we'll try the flea-flicker. Let's go! Break!"

Before Waterbury knew what happened, Chip struck quickly with two short passes from the spread and advanced the ball to the Blues' twenty-eight.

He had hit Cody Collins with the first one for a three-yard gain and then had faked an end run to hold up the charging line as he connected with Red Schwartz kneeling nine yards behind the Waterbury defender. Chip had rifled that last pass! The Big Reds were charging! The ball rested on the Waterbury twenty-eight-yard line, first down, ten yards to go.

THE FLEA-FLICKER

While Chip whispered his directions in the Valley Falls huddle, two men, more than a hundred miles away, huddled on either side of a small radio. Doc Jones and John Schroeder, studies in concentration, strained to catch the announcer's every word.

The voice of Stan Gomez came over the air.

"Timeout, folks. It's second and ten again. They're in the huddle—now they're coming out. They're lining up in Rockwell's new formation. Hilton is back—there's the snap. Hilton is running to the left—he's going to run the ball. No! He's going to pass—he throws—Williams catches it! He pivots around—he's tackled—he's going down—he FUMBLES!

"No, I'm wrong! Williams didn't fumble, folks. It was a lateral back to a Big Red lineman. It's number 66. Number 66 is running toward the west corner of the field. It's Soapy Smith—he's breaking away! Can he score? He's at the fifteen—the ten—the five—he's OVER!

"Valley Falls scores! The Big Reds just scored on a lateral from Ted Williams to Soapy Smith, and Valley Falls now leads six to nothing here in the last few seconds of the third quarter. Didn't I tell you, Casey, didn't I tell you Rockwell would have something in his playbook!"

Down on the sideline in front of the Valley Falls bench, Coach Henry Rockwell was on his feet staring in amazement at Chip Hilton and his Big Red teammates.

"Where did they dig that up?" he kept saying to no one in particular. Rockwell's confusion was shared by Chet Stewart and Bill Thomas. They were speechless.

Not so the team of happy teenagers on the field. They pounded Soapy, Chip, and Ted Williams unmercifully. Soapy thrust his chest out a mile and leaned this way and that, trying to get as many punches as possible; this was his big moment.

The referee finally got it across to the celebrating Big Reds that the game wasn't over, and there was a little matter of a penalty coming up if they didn't get on with the game. Fortunately, Speed Morris dashed in just then to report for Jordan Taylor and to hold the ball for Chip's try for the extra point. So the Big Reds settled down long enough to see Chip send the ball through the uprights for his ninth straight conversion. Right after the kick, Rockwell sent Taylor back in for Morris.

The referee *had* been wrong though. The game *was* over as far as further scoring was concerned. The Blues didn't have a chance. They were stunned by the sudden change of the VF tempo. The Big Reds were satisfied to play it safe and protect that seven-point margin. That was the way it ended: Valley Falls 7, Waterbury 0.

After the game, no one could get near the Valley Falls bus without a struggle. The players pushed through the crowd to the bus. There they were met by Petey Jackson and Dink Davis. Fans hoisted players on their shoulders for everyone to see and cheer.

Soapy timed his arrival just right; he arrived last, just as he had planned.

"Speech! Speech!" the boisterous crowd yelled. Soapy, with a smile spanning his rosy, freckled face, was hoisted onto the hood of the bus by Petey and Dink. Then he told the crowd just how *he* had won the game.

"You see," he said, leaning over and speaking confidentially to the laughing crowd, "you see, it was like this. On the way over, Rock, that's the coach, you know, Rock says to me, 'Now what do you think we ought to do this afternoon, Smith?' Well, you know how I am, sorta retiring and modest-like. Well, I always liked the Rock. He's not a bad guy. So I says, 'Well, Rock, if it was me, I'd try a new formation.' So he says, 'OK, Smith, you take charge!'

"Well, you know the kind of a guy I am!" Soapy chuckled and sputtered, enjoying himself immensely. "I don't want any undue recognition, nothing like a knighthood or anything, but, well, you all saw what happened. But, I'd just as soon someone else got a *little* of the credit."

Suddenly, laughing players scrambled for their favorite seats in the bus for the ride home as Rockwell, Rogers, Stewart, and Thomas came pushing their way through the cheering crowd. Just as the driver closed the doors, Petey Jackson blandly addressed a question to everyone within hearing: "Say, what size tires does this bus have?"

"Is this another football quiz question? What do you care?" Miguel Rodriguez challenged.

"Oh, I don't care," Petey said cheerfully. "Only I wonder if anyone else noticed Fats Ohlsen is having tire trouble. Look! Of all the tough luck! Someone let the air out of all four of poor Ohlsen's tires and threw all the little valve stems away!"

CHAPTER 13

An Understanding Man

CHIP GROPED along the fence in the dark until he came to the hole. Then he pushed his way through the swinging boards and stood with his back pressed against the cold wall while he surveyed the deserted shipping and receiving yard. Slipping carefully from one dark shadow to another, he headed for the fourth window of the mixing room and gently pushed it inward. He waited there for a second and then hoisted himself to one knee on the sill and dropped noiselessly into the big mixing room.

The plant was deathly quiet. Only the "whir-clop" of a massive agitator could be heard pulsating through the silence. It was number three, the agitator the last of the bad clay had come from. The others, one and two, were not in use.

Chip tiptoed toward the packing case that he and his surveillance team had been hiding behind all through the week. "Maybe I can slip up on him," he whispered to himself. But when he arrived within a few feet of the box, a tall, shadowy bulk rose silently in the semidarkness. It was Biggie.

"You're worn out, aren't you, Chip?" Cohen whispered, worried about his friend. "Think you can make it? Want me to stay with you?"

To all of Biggie's questions Chip gave an emphatic, "No!" This was *his* watch, and he meant to take it.

After Biggie left, Chip made himself comfortable in the shadow of the box. He was glad he had worn a sweater and his dad's old varsity jacket. There was a decided chill in the air; winter was not too far away—neither was basketball.

Chip had never tried to analyze just why he had such a keen interest in George Browning, but the thought of playing basketball brought the answer. He really loved the game and knew how much it could mean to Taps. Besides, Mr. Browning had been a victim, and someone was to blame. But maybe all this detective business was foolish. Maybe he should have forgotten the whole thing . . . let it work itself out.

A little later, he heard Cal Bender's steady pace as he made his rounds. Bender visited every security checkpoint station once every hour. It was a comforting thought. Outside, in the plant yard, Sam McQueen had the same responsibility. Chip had heard him whistling several times as he made his tour of the outside watch stops.

Chip was comfortably warm now and just a bit drowsy. *Here, this is no good . . . wake up . . . gotta stay alert.* He shifted his cramped legs and leaned forward to get a better view of the two approaches to the number-three agitator. The lights in the halls were dim, and there were several shadows that his imagination tried to form into the outline of a man.

The time passed slowly. Again and again, Chip caught himself dozing off. Suddenly, he sat up with a start! Cold chills ran the length of his spine, and the hair on the back of his head tingled as though standing on end. A tightness constricted his forehead just below the scalp line, and his heart beat wildly in his ears. He listened intently, straining in the silence.

Again, the unusual sound that had registered in his half-consciousness and snapped him out of his catnap broke the silence. All of Chip's faculties were alert now, and his heart seemed to thump right against the lining of his jacket. He glanced at the shadows in the hallways. They were still there—still shifting a bit, but the sound had not come from that direction. He turned his eyes to the window through which he had entered the plant, but that was tightly closed.

He heard the sound again! This time there was no question about the direction. It was directly behind him. He sat as if paralyzed while he tried to figure out whether there was a window there. He pushed back against the wall and turned his eyes up as far as possible without moving his head. There *was* a window, right behind him. Someone *was* trying to get it open! Then he heard soft footsteps move along the wall to the next window. He breathed a short sigh of relief. That was close!

Now what? He'd been looking forward to a moment like this, and here it was, and he didn't know what he was going to do. Maybe it was Speed or Biggie or Abe. He dismissed the hopeful thought immediately.

One thing was sure; he wasn't going to move, unless that someone out there came in and fooled around the agitator. He focused his eyes on the fourth window; it moved upward . . . and opened! A blundering leg came through first, followed by a bulky body. The man crouching there in the shadows took a long time to get his bearings, and Chip nervously flexed his muscles and tried to plan his course of action. He was sure of one thing: the man who had come through the window was there for no good.

The bulky figure moved slowly toward the agitator, keeping in the shadows. When he reached the number three, he paused and glanced cautiously in all directions. Here, the glow from the big center lamp cast its brightest shaft of light, and Chip got a good look at the man who stood there fumbling at his coat pocket.

Chip carefully drew his feet up under his body. One course of action was imperative—he must prevent that man from throwing anything into the big agitator!

The man drew a closed hand out of his pocket and glanced at the top of the agitator. Chip waited no longer. With a wild yell, he bounded halfway across the space that separated the two and grappled with the surprised visitor. The intruder was hurled to his knees by the sudden attack, but there Chip's advantage swiftly ended. Although the man's gasping breath reeked with alcohol, he was far from handicapped by its influence. Cursing and in panic, the man wrenched free and cracked Chip on the back of the head. Chip felt consciousness leaving him. The blow had been only a glancing one, but Chip had never felt a hand so hard. He drove forward and grasped the man's knees, trying to tackle him to the floor. The strength wilted from Chip's arms, and the desperate man easily pushed Chip to the floor.

As the half-conscious teenager struggled to regain his feet, he glimpsed something shiny that flashed in the light and was held in a powerful fist. Chip ducked and caught the paralyzing blow on his shoulder. The pain shooting down his back was almost unbearable, but he managed a desperate "Help!"

Almost as if the cry had released a switch, the plant siren shrieked in warning wails and the emergency lights flashed on, illuminating every square foot of the plant, inside and out. The pounding of running feet echoed as the man kicked at Chip's face and sprinted for the window. Chip crawled up on his knees and started in pursuit. This guy wasn't going to get away now!

Just as Cal Bender came stumbling up, the window was smashed open from the outside, and Abe Cohen hurtled through.

"Watch out, Abe!" Chip shouted. "Watch his right hand!"

Cohen's eyes flashed toward Chip, then back to his vicious adversary's hand, and then he began a slow, determined advance.

"So, Bracken," he grated, "it was you all the time. I thought it was!" Then he hurled himself forward. Bracken didn't have a chance. Having caught sight of Chip's bloodied face, Abe Cohen was now filled with cold rage.

Bracken tried to hit the charging tornado, but his steel-encased fist jabbed harmlessly over a powerful shoulder, and he was smashed to the floor under a flurry of blows. The steel knuckles went flying across the concrete floor. Abe picked Bracken up as though he were a child and, holding him by the collar with his left hand, smashed a hard right to the frantic caster's jaw. That was the clincher!

Cohen let him sag to the floor. "You lie down on that floor and stay there," he seethed ominously through clenched teeth. "And keep your arms out wide too." He turned to Bender.

"Call J. P. and the police! Hurry!"

As Bender scurried away, Sam McQueen and a group of other men came running down the hall. "What's going on here?" McQueen gasped. "What's the trouble?"

Cohen pointed to Bracken. "There's the trouble," he declared. "There's the guy that caused *all* the trouble!"

"You mean the mix?"

"That's right!"

"What *hit* him?" one of the breathless men asked.

"Abe hit him," Chip said admiringly as he wiped the blood from the side of his mouth.

"What are you doing here? How'd you get in here? And, what hit *you?*" drilled McQueen, looking at Chip's bloody face.

"Those steel knuckles over there," said Cohen, nodding toward the vicious weapon. "But don't touch them. I want the police to find them right there where they are."

An hour later, Chip and Abe sat in J. P. Ohlsen's office while a police officer took notes on their part in the night's events. Bracken had been hustled off to jail after he had confessed. At first, he had professed ignorance about the mix. But after Chip had pointed to the scattered copper filings on the stone floor beneath the agitator and the police had discovered the most damaging evidence of all—the remaining copper filings in his coat pocket—he had admitted his guilt.

Biggie and Speed leaned against the window sill and watched everything with wide-awake eyes. They had heard the siren and had joined about everybody in town, it seemed, in hurrying to the pottery. Cal Bender and Sam McQueen had already gone back to the plant, and everything was quiet again. Abe explained that he had been suspicious of Bracken ever since he had caught a hidden meaning in Bracken's words one night in Sorelli's. Cohen looked at J. P. with a little embarrassment when he spoke about Mike's, but Ohlsen's expression remained unchanged.

That particular night, Abe continued, the pottery workers had been discussing the bad ware, and Bracken had said, "Yeah, and there'll be more too." Abe had been trailing Bracken every night since.

Tonight, after Sorelli's closed, Abe had followed Bracken again. He had nearly given up, though, for the ugly-dispositioned caster had started straight home. Just when Abe was about to turn around and go home, too, Bracken had suddenly wheeled about and started for the pottery.

When he finished, Abe was still a bit confused. "You know, Mr. Ohlsen," he said, "there's one thing I can't figure out yet. Why did Bracken want to spoil the ware?"

"I think I know the answer to that, Abe," J. P. said thoughtfully. "Several weeks ago I was checking the spoiled ware slips, and I noticed the name Tom Bracken turned up most consistently for bad ware. I didn't know the fellow, so I sent for Gordon Pinder and asked him to bring Bracken along.

"I didn't like Bracken's antagonistic attitude even then, and, when his reaction to my criticism about the bad ware was defiant, I flatly told him his work would have to improve or I'd fire him."

After the police officer left, Chip decided now was the time to say what had been on his mind ever since J. P. had asked him up to the office.

"Say, Mr. Ohlsen," he began, "I was won—"

AN UNDERSTANDING MAN

J. P. laughed. "I know," he said, "you're wondering when George Browning can come back to work. Right away, of course! Tell him to report back to his supervisory position tomorrow morning. How are you after Bracken roughed you up?"

"I'll be OK. But Mr. Browning isn't home, Mr. Ohlsen. He's working over in Steeltown."

"Well, another week won't hurt. Tell him to give his boss a week's notice and report next Monday. OK?"

"Yes, sir! I wish I could tell him the good news right away."

"Call him."

"He doesn't have a phone."

"Well, then, send him a letter. Have you got his address?"

"Yes, sir. I've got a letter from him right here in my pocket."

"All right, good. Type what you want to say."

Chip sat down at Carolyn Wenzel's computer and, with Biggie and Speed leaning over the back of the chair, typed out the message.

```
GOOD NEWS! EVERYTHING CLEARED UP.
IMPORTANT YOU MEET ME AT SUGAR
BOWL AT SEVEN P.M. SATURDAY, NOV.
11. KEEP CONFIDENTIAL. LETTER FOL-
LOWS. BIG SURPRISE AWAITING YOU!
            CHIP HILTON
```

J. P. smiled as he read the typed words. "I'll see to it that Mrs. Wenzel sends your note out first thing in the morning by express mail. Make you feel better?"

"Yes, now I can go home and get some sleep!" said Chip.

TOUCHDOWN PASS

As Abe, Biggie, and Chip piled into the Mustang, Speed had a sudden thought. "Hey, Mr. Ohlsen never even got wise to the hole in the fence when the police asked Bracken how he got in, remember? Bracken said two or three times he came in through the hole."

"Guess J. P. had too many other things on his mind," volunteered Biggie.

Abe laughed. "That's what you think!" he said. "J. P. never misses a trick! I've been trying to tell you Sherlocks that J. P. Ohlsen is an understanding man. Why, he probably put the hinges on the boards and tested it a few times himself!"

CHAPTER 14

Gossip Columnist

CHIP'S HEAD bobbed up and down behind the case as he polished the chrome finish. Every once in a while, he peered toward the long fountain where Speed, Soapy, and Red Schwartz had Petey Jackson cornered. Chip convulsed with laughter as his three friends fired one football trivia question after another at the self-proclaimed sports historian.

Petey stammered and looked helplessly from one tormentor to the other. "Aw, cut it out, you guys. I never said I knew the answers to all those questions—"

"You *never!*" Speed regarded Petey in amazement. "How about the time I was askin' you those questions? The time Biggie won! How come you knew the answers that time?"

Chip leaned on the counter and watched Petey squirm. He knew the answer to that one. He, too, had wondered how Petey could rattle off the answers so confidently. He had noticed Petey was always juggling a long soda spoon whenever anyone asked him about the questions.

Petey was an expert juggler of spoons, glasses, plates, and even ice-cream cones. Chip had seen others flip ice cream from a scoop downward into a cone, but Petey was the only person he had ever seen who could flip a scoop of ice cream up in the air from a scoop and catch it in the cone. Chip knew there had to be a trick in that maneuver, but he could never figure it out.

He'd figured out the solution to Petey's ready answers to the football questions though. One time, when Petey had been answering one question after another, Chip had noticed he frequently dropped the long spoon after twirling it into the air. That was unlike Petey.

Chip had quietly slipped up behind him, and there, on a big piece of cardboard taped beneath the counter top, cleverly out of sight, was a card on which the football quiz master had written the answers. Chip hadn't let on he had seen the card then; now he waited for Petey's explanation.

Petey was trapped. He knew this threesome well. Woe, indeed, if he got on the wrong side of this crew. He decided to come clean with the truth about everything.

"Oh, what's the use! You guys are too smart. OK, I didn't know the answers to the questions. I asked the Rock to help me out. He gave me the questions and answers and a rule book. See?" Petey held up a well-worn rule book as evidence.

Soapy howled. "Well, what d'ya know about that? So Rock was behind it all the time! No wonder you had the right answers." He had a sudden inspiration. "Hey! What if we could pull one over on Rock and trick him into a mistake. Let's try it!"

Petey breathed a sigh of relief and rolled his big blue eyes toward the ceiling. But his freedom didn't last long. As he turned back toward the fountain, he met the shrewd, appraising gaze of Red Schwartz. Red's green-flecked eyes were coldly demanding.

Petey knew what that meant. "What'll you guys have?" he managed. "Treat's on me, you know."

"Yeah, we know," echoed Soapy.

"And we want to see it rung up on the register too," added Speed.

Chip strolled up. "Count me in too," he declared. "I haven't eaten for days!"

Petey groaned. "OK," he said weakly, "but you guys gotta promise not to tell anyone about Rock givin' me the questions. OK?"

"Why?" demanded Speed.

"Because, well, because I've got a new quiz all made up and—"

Four protesting voices cut him short. "No! Not another one!"

"No sir, nothing doing!"

"Enough's enough!"

Petey held up both hands and quieted the protests. "I know, guys, I know. But this is different. This one isn't historical, technical, or about sports trivia. It's one of those gossip-column-type things. Come on, you guys, be sports. Promise you won't say anything until after this week, OK?"

He picked up an ice-cream scoop and twirled it suggestively.

TOUCHDOWN PASS

Four pairs of eyes met and four heads nodded in solemn unison as Petey grimly prepared eight double sundaes with whipped cream, cherries, nuts, and chocolate syrup. Shades of Rockwell!

It seemed as though everything had been right . . . *this* week.

On his way home from church, Chip had picked up another newspaper while Mrs. Hilton talked with friends about the pottery incident. She reassured everyone that Chip was fine.

At home, Chip told his mother about the night's events for the umpteenth time. Joe Kennedy of the *Times* and Pete Williams of the *Post* had called and interviewed him about his part in the pottery investigation. Monday's papers had carried front-page stories of the case. Chip had felt foolish. Both writers had given a mystery twist to their articles and made near-heroes of Biggie, Speed, and himself. Abe hadn't gotten half the credit he deserved. If it hadn't been for Abe, there wouldn't have been a good ending to the story.

There had been no practice on Monday, but on Tuesday, Rockwell had called Biggie and Speed into his office and told them he was sorry he had doubted them. He had seen them going down toward the Academy on their way to the pottery at a late hour several times during the past week and had found it impossible to understand why they were out so late. That was the reason for the pregame speech at Waterbury.

Then, out on the field, the Rock had complimented the whole team for its cleverness in setting up the flea-flicker. He'd said the Big Reds had what it took to be champions—state champions.

GOSSIP COLUMNIST

On Wednesday, Chip received a letter from George Browning. Browning wrote he had given notice to his employer and would meet Chip on Saturday night at seven o'clock at the Sugar Bowl. He said he was curious about Chip's Saturday night plans, but he promised to keep the whole matter to himself.

Today's practice had been the best of the season. Speed's ankle was back in shape; he would be able to play Saturday against Delford. The squad had been full of drive and confidence.

If the Big Reds defeated Delford, they'd be tied with Steeltown for the leadership of Section Two. The next two games were at home: Rutledge from Section Four on November 25 and the big game with Steeltown on December 2.

Maybe there would be a postseason game for the state championship if they won all the rest. Maybe they would have a chance to be in the mythical state championship if they ended up the only undefeated team in the state.

Chip's thoughts were rudely interrupted by Petey's high-pitched voice. "Come on, Chip. Hurry up before the place gets swamped. Don't you want to see the new quiz?" Petey was impatient.

Chip looked up in surprise. He'd forgotten where he was. He looked at his friends' plates in pretended amazement.

"Soapy, what did you do with all that?"

"What did *you* do with all that?" Soapy retorted.

Chip looked down at his own plates. He had polished off both of them. "Well, what do you know about that!" he said.

TOUCHDOWN PASS

"Look what I found," Petey announced mischievously. He pulled the latest quiz card out from under the counter and held it up for his now-satisfied customers' inspection.

There was silence for a few moments; then Soapy jumped alive with energy. "Oh man! Wait until everyone sees this!" He turned to Petey and held out his hand. "Congratulations, Petey! You've got something here. Now you're *really* dishing it out!"

PETEY JACKSON'S
FINAL (maybe) FOOTBALL QUIZ
WIN A PRIZE

1. Who let the air out of Fats Ohlsen's tires at the Waterbury game?
2. Where was Coach Rockwell between halves of the Nov. 4 game?
3. What great football authority provided the questions and answers for the previous questions?
4. What transpired in Coach Rockwell's office when three prominent South Side athletes were called on the carpet?
5. What happened when the "Battle of the Locker Room" was discussed in Mr. Zimmerman's office?
6. What Chip Hilton protégé may create history on the VF hardcourt?
7. What player disregarded Coach Rockwell's orders and saved VF from defeat?
8. Who calls Speed Morris every Sunday morning and for what reason?
9. How old is Pop Brown? How long has he been the trainer at Valley Falls? What did he do before coming to VF?
10. What prominent person in VF once won a game for the Big Reds by scoring for the other team?

CHAPTER 15

Bootleg Play

ROCKWELL RINGED the four circles representing the eligible pass receivers with heavy borders and laid the marker in the tray below the portable whiteboard. He turned slowly and faced the players seated in the gymnasium bleachers.

"Boys, I haven't used a spread formation for years. But what you did last Saturday from punt formation, with your ends and halfbacks out, had me thinking all week. The sportswriters gave me credit for that one, but I guess we know who was responsible for that—and I want to compliment you right now, Chip, for fast thinking and great execution of your plays." He turned and regarded Soapy Smith with a smile. "And I want you to know, Smith, that I never saw anyone run any faster than you did when you took that lateral from Williams— not even Speed Morris."

Soapy sat up taller, his freckled face animated with pride.

"But," continued Rockwell, "wasn't the play set up for Collins?"

Soapy's smile sagged, his face flushed a violent red, and he slowly sank back on the bleacher seat.

"Wasn't it?" persisted Rockwell.

"It was, Coach," interrupted Cody Collins. "It *was* set up for me, but it's a good thing Soapy was there. I got flattened before I ever got near Williams."

Everyone turned to look at Collins in surprise. It was the first time he had ever made any sort of a positive comment toward one of Chip's friends. Now Williams broke in. The big, quiet senior seldom spoke unless addressed by someone.

"Cody's right, Coach," he said. "When I pivoted around to pass the ball back to Cody, he wasn't in sight. Then I saw Soapy come tearing out of the line to lead interference for Cody, and I just threw it in his direction and prayed. I don't know yet how he caught the ball. It was a terrible pass."

Soapy's face lit up again, and he looked gratefully at Collins and Williams. He had a wide grin as he turned back to look at Rockwell, who winked at him and hooked a thumb at the board.

"Well, however that all happened, we're going to have a spread formation to add to our repertory, starting right now. Maybe we won't need it for Delford tomorrow, now that Speed's back in shape, but we might. This formation has greater possibilities, by far, than the one you created on Saturday." He turned and studied the outline on the board.

"I've placed the initials of the starting eleven in the positions they will take, and each of you will have to master your respective assignments out on the field this

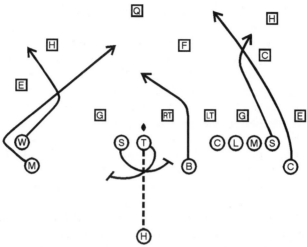

afternoon. I know this is short notice, but there isn't a great deal to learn—you can do it. The biggest part of the responsibility belongs to the passer. That's you, Hilton. The passer is back from ten to twelve yards. This man has to be a strong thrower and a hard runner, and that's the chief reason I decided to give the spread a try— because you're perfect for that position, Hilton.

"Smith and Trullo, S and T, will play in the middle, and you are both expected to block for the passer. All other linemen—C, L, M—Cohen, Leonard, and Mazotta, will run interference on running plays and block for the passer, if possible, on pass plays. At the snap, we'll have at least seven men on the line of scrimmage. Linemen, remember, you can't do any downfield blocking until the receiver has caught the ball. Also, after the ball is ready for play, each player must have been within fifteen yards of the ball before the snap. Now, Hilton, suppose you tell us what we can do from the spread."

TOUCHDOWN PASS

Chip said the formation was especially strong for passes because the receivers—the two ends, the two half-backs, and the fullback—were spread nearly the width of the field. All were in good position to break into receiving territory. The formation was suitable for running plays too. The passer could run to the right and pick up his interference.

"How about the blocking assignment for a play like that?"

"Well," Chip continued, "if they lined up as you have drawn there, Soapy could take the defensive man marked RT. Chris and Biggie could double-team defensive LT. The rest of the line—L, M, and S—could block anyone almost. Guess it would be better if they just formed a wedge and took anyone who tried to break through."

"Now, boys," Rockwell continued, "I've shown the paths the pass receivers might follow in trying to get free, but keep in mind there is no set path for you to follow. We haven't got time to develop buttonhooks and other types of play passes. We'll just have to depend upon Chip to find the open receiver. Receivers, you help your quarterback connect when you come back to get the pass—don't wait for the ball to come to you. Any questions?" He erased the formation and again faced the squad.

Coach Rockwell turned to find Biggie Cohen on his feet.

"You seem to have a question, Biggie. What is it?" inquired the coach.

"Coach, you," stammered Cohen, "you told us you were going to describe the Statue of Liberty play and—"

Rockwell smiled. "Right you are, Biggie. I should have brought it up in one of our sessions before this. Of course, you know the Statue of Liberty is an old play to keep in reserve for a time when everything is exactly right for it. It's a scoring play and will go best when a pass or two has clicked and the defensive ends are charging in to rush the passer.

"Everybody's got to fake—passer, receivers, and blockers. Set it up for Morris around right end. Speed, when you get that ball, you make it around that right end as hard as you can go. Understand?

"Everyone pay attention now. I'll put the Statue of Liberty play up here on the board so everyone can see just what takes place."

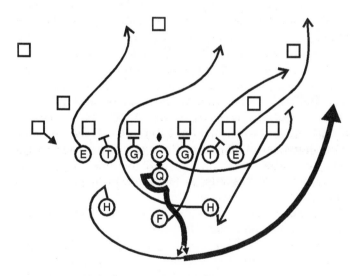

"On the snap, the right halfback crosses in front of the fullback and drives between left guard and left tackle. The fullback delays and, after the right halfback cuts by him, drives over right guard and down the field. The quarterback fakes to both and then runs back to his usual passing position and cocks his arm for a pass.

"The left halfback, Morris, takes two, three steps forward, delays for a count of two, and then cuts behind the quarterback and takes the ball off of his hand and heads for the right flank.

"I want to see some proper downfield blocking! Our center chases the defensive back and keeps after him—he's dangerous!

"Now, if the defensive ends wise up and if they fail to charge in on the play to rush the passer, you've got to go get them, or they'll smear this play for a big loss.

"We'll have just a light workout this afternoon—chiefly signals, a little passing, and a little kicking. Tomorrow, we play Delford. We'll leave here at 11:30. However, I want everyone here no later than 10:45. We'll eat together after the game.

"Delford's a great sports town. They play hard over there, especially against Valley Falls. The crowd is strictly hometown. You'll have to fight and fight hard to win—but you can do it. Just keep your heads, play clean, and forget the crowd.

"Burrell Rogers tells me there is to be a Veterans Day ceremony on the school steps tomorrow morning at eleven o'clock, so let's be here promptly. All right, let's have a snappy half-hour workout."

The Sugar Bowl was jammed that night. Everybody was talking about Petey's quiz and the journey to Delford. Although Rockwell hadn't mentioned it, every player on the squad and practically every sports fan in Valley Falls knew about the intense feeling between Rockwell and the big, blustering, red-faced Jinx Jenkins, coach of the Delford High School football team.

Before he knew it, Chip and the team were aboard the Valley Falls bus on the way to Delford. As Chip watched the scenery pass by the window, his thoughts alternated between the game and George Browning.

Last night Chip and Petey had completed the plans for the surprise party to celebrate the reinstatement of George Browning in his pottery position. The party was going to be held at the Hilton home, and Petey had volunteered to take care of refreshments. Chip's plan was to slip George Browning into the house and then invite Mrs. Browning, Taps, and Suzy over for the big surprise.

J. P. Ohlsen had given Chip a letter telling George Browning his old job was waiting, and he had enclosed a check for the job time he had missed. Mary Hilton was as enthusiastic as Chip over the party plans. Chip was to meet Mr. Browning and Petey at the Sugar Bowl at seven o'clock. Chip had wanted to ask Biggie, Speed, and Abe to come along, but Mary Hilton was concerned a crowd might be embarrassing to the Brownings. They had decided to make it a gathering for just the two families and Petey.

The Veterans Day remembrance that morning on the school steps had been impressive, and the orchestra had played several selections. At exactly eleven o'clock everyone had stood with bowed and uncovered heads for a minute of silence. The solemn memorial exercise had sombered the squad. After the bus was on the road to Delford, fifty miles away, the tenor had changed, and gradually the lilting spirit of a winning ball club became evident.

TOUCHDOWN PASS

It was a beautiful day for football, clear and cool. There was just enough of a tang in the air to make a player's blood surge and make him impatient to get going. Speed and Chip stood in the center of the Delford High School athletic field while a terrific din filled the field.

As Chip stood in the little huddle before the toss, he glanced at the home bench and focused his eyes on the aggressive Delford coach. Jenkins stood near the sidelines, watching the circle with impatient eyes. Without turning his head, Chip knew the Rock would be standing in an almost identical pose and with just as much impatience. Why, he wondered, did the two coaches feel so bitterly toward each other? Why couldn't they have an armistice?

Chip and Speed won the toss and elected to receive. The kick was low and short. Badger took the ball on Valley Falls's twenty-five and dug straight up the field to the thirty-eight. On the first play of the game, Chip faked to Speed, pivoted, and, after Collins cut by, gave Badger a perfect handoff. Chris found a hole and drove to the forty-five. It was second and three for a first down.

On the next play, Chip tossed the ball to Speed for what was supposed to be a dive play into the line for a first down, but the tricky scatback broke away and dashed to the Delford forty-yard line. It was a beautiful run, the kind of explosive sprint only Speed Morris could produce. The fans were barely settled in their seats after the kickoff, and Valley Falls was already in Delford territory! Delford called a timeout.

When play resumed, Chip called the same play, and Speed again raced for a first down, placing the ball on the Delford twenty-eight-yard line. Speed was tackled near the sideline, and while the official carried the ball to the hash marks, a new substitute for the Delford right tackle spot entered the game with instructions from Jenkins.

Chip wasted no time in the huddle. The Rock had always said, "When you have an opponent on the run—keep him on the run."

"OK, men, it's time for the bootleg with a pass to Speed into their secondary. Fake cross buck; pass to Speed in the center. Good fakes needed. Break!"

Trullo's long arms swept the ball back. Chip pivoted to his left, held the ball in his stomach with his left hand, faked a handoff to Speed with his right hand, continued his turn, and faked to Collins. Chris, hunched over and arms crossed as if covering the ball, sliced into the line. Then Chip followed his usual path, taking four long steps to the rear, all the time keeping the ball covered. On the fourth step, he jabbed his right foot into the ground and turned to look for Speed.

Speed was just cutting into the open area. He had faked the Delford right defensive back completely off balance.

Chip tossed a perfect pass, shoulder high, and with just enough lead to force Speed to cut down the middle and away from the Delford left defensive back, who was heading desperately for the elusive speedster.

Speed took the ball almost over his shoulder and cut straight toward the goal line. The Delford safety, at his own twelve-yard line, set his sights on Morris. Speed never slowed his pace as he approached the on-coming tackler. The wary safety made the mistake of hesitating. That was all Speed needed. He juked to the right and, just as the tackler committed, turned so easily the diving safety never even touched the tantalizing leg he was aiming for. The tricky speedster crossed the goal line standing up.

With Speed holding, Chip kicked the extra point, and Valley Falls led 7–0. The touchdown had come so easily that the Big Reds rooters chanted "Roll 'em up! Roll 'em up!"

But it wasn't going to be that easy. Delford received and, as often happens when an opposing team has scored easily, took advantage of the Big Reds' satisfaction to run the kickoff back to midfield. There, the Delford team launched a vicious drive through the line with its wing formation, gaining three, five, three, five, two, three, and four yards with monotonous precision. Despite Chip's two timeouts during this drive, Delford was not to be denied and scored. Valley Falls 7, Delford 7.

As the Big Reds readied to receive the kickoff, Badger moved to Chip's side. "Take my place back on the ten, Chip," he said. "You're a better runner than me, and I'll give you some interference."

Chip nodded in surprised agreement. What a change the past few weeks had made in the attitude of the South Side crowd. The Big Reds were a team now.

The kick was high, and Chip took the ball in full stride on the fifteen and followed Badger. He was brought down hard on the forty. It was a good, solid return as Badger and Hilton worked well together. But the offensive attack stalled.

Chip tried Speed on the quick-opening play that had been so effective before, but Delford was ready for Morris and stopped him cold. Chip tried to hold Delford in check by punting, trying to outkick the opponents. But Delford wanted to run the ball and did. Just before the end of the half, Delford scored and kicked the extra point. Delford 14, Valley Falls 7.

Back in Valley Falls, Doc Jones and John Schroeder hunched over the little radio in the office above the Sugar Bowl.

"Yes, folks, Delford has just scored on straight, hard-running football. This is the second touchdown Delford has punched through the Big Red line. Valley Falls also took their last timeout of the half in a failed effort to stop Delford's punishing ground attack. That running attack is reminiscent of Rockwell's team last year. The Big Reds were always a power team, you know.

"Well, Valley Falls is going to receive again. The score now is Delford 14, Valley Falls 7. The Big Reds started a little too fast—maybe the easy score tempted them to relax.

"And now, here's John Humphrey."

"Thanks, Stan. Folks, you've been listening to Valley Falls's own Stan Gomez. He'll be back on the air in just a few minutes to bring you a review of this first half.

"There's the kick. It's a long, high one. Down to the Falls ten. Morris has it. Delford's converging on the five-foot-ten-inch speedster. Morris is up to the twenty—the twenty-five—the thirty—the thirty-five, and he's finally brought down. It took about half the Delford team to halt Morris. It'll be Valley Falls's ball, first and ten, on about the thirty-seven. Wait a second.

"There's something wrong down there! The Delford players are up, but there's a Valley Falls player still on the ground. It looks like Morris. It *is* Morris!

"There goes the Falls trainer out on the field. He's working near Morris's ankle. The trainer is now standing and has called for assistance. They're bringing him out of the game. Yes, Valley Falls's star runner is being carried off the field.

"Fans, you know Speed Morris, Valley Falls's All-State halfback, has been on the sidelines for the past three weeks with a bad ankle. Let's hope it's not serious.

"Time is in again with Jordan Taylor replacing Morris. Hilton's at the quarterback spot. There's the snap from center. Hilton is—no—it looked like Hilton faked a pass and now he's running around his own left end. He's going wide, clear across the field, but he isn't going to get anywhere. There's the tackle—he's down on the other side of the field.

"There's only fifty seconds left to play in this half and no timeouts for Falls. Hilton is watching the clock. He's trying to use all the time possible. He can't risk losing the ball and allowing another Delford score.

"Hilton runs again—there's the whistle—no gain. Third down and twelve to go. Hilton hands to Taylor. He's stopped immediately at the line. Looks like the Big Reds will have to kick.

"Falls is in punt formation. There's the snap—Hilton kicks it—it's a high one! This kid can really boot that leather. This one will give his coverage team time to get down the field.

"Pilsner is signaling for a fair catch. He catches it. Look out! I thought he might have trouble with that catch. Pilsner was surrounded by the Big Reds' ends and that human bulldozer, Biggie Cohen. That was smart. Pilsner signaled for a fair catch because he was surrounded with no chance of advancing the ball, and he knew they would have time for one play. There's ten seconds left to play.

BOOTLEG PLAY

"It's Delford's ball, on their own thirty-five-yard line. They'll probably pass. There goes the snap from center. Pilsner is running back—he's going to pass—"

Out on the field, Chip backed up. He couldn't allow anyone to get behind him on this play. A long gain wouldn't matter; this was the last play of the half.

Two Delford receivers tried to get by Chip. Pilsner faded back to his own twenty-five before releasing the ball in a long, desperate throw down the field toward Hilton.

The three players went up in a tangle of leaping figures, but Chip's last split-second lunge meant the difference. His long fingers met the ball just as he had often done in basketball, and he flipped the ball to the ground. The half was over. The score: Delford 14, Valley Falls 7.

In the dressing room, Pop worked furiously on Speed's ankle. Chip leaned back against the wall, his long legs outstretched, resting. Woe, indeed, to the player who did not take advantage of every one of the fifteen precious intermission minutes for complete relaxation. That was one of Rockwell's pet training principles.

After five minutes of quiet, Coach Rockwell gave his second-half instructions. When he finished, Speed spoke up. "I'm all right, Coach," he said. "Honest! My ankle feels fine now. On that tackle their whole team piled on it! That won't happen again." He shook his head grimly. "Guess I should have taped up the good leg!"

Rockwell grasped Chip's arm and walked with him out to the field for the second half. "It looks like we'll have to take to the air to beat this team, Chip," he said earnestly. "Use your own judgment about the spread. I'm sure you can hurt them with that. It's too bad you don't have Speed in there to receive, but Schwartz and Collins can get the job done."

"What *about* Speed, Coach?"

"We can't take a chance on it, Chip. We'll try it without him!" He gave Chip a parting slap on the back. "Go get 'em, Chipper!"

Delford prepared to receive as the official's whistle to resume play silenced the crowd. Chip booted a long one back to the ten. Biggie hit the ball carrier hard on the twenty-two and solicitously helped him to his feet. Biggie's lips curled in a half-smile, but his eyes were not smiling. Biggie hadn't forgotten the Delford piling-on that resulted in a seat on the bench for Speed.

The third quarter was a football nightmare. The frenzied crowd was on its feet from the start to the end. Delford was checked on the forty and kicked to Chip on the Valley Falls twenty-five-yard stripe.

On a fake punt, Chip broke free around right end and twisted and fought his way to the Delford forty-five. There, he alternated Chris Badger and Cody Collins on straight line hits that carried to the Delford fifteen before the attack stalled. On fourth down and four to go, Chip knocked down a wobbly three pointer to make the score Delford 14, Valley Falls 10.

Delford received, and once more the Big Reds dug in—and held too. Then Chip hit Ted Williams with a thirty-yard pass, and they were knocking on Delford's door for a score. But the Big Reds had spent themselves and could not gain. On fourth down, Chip had split the uprights with another field goal. Jordan had been nervous and had tilted the ball too far back; it had been a lucky hit.

BOOTLEG PLAY

Delford's running attack was still clicking and before the quarter ended, Delford punched over two more touchdowns but missed both conversions. The score at the end of the third quarter: Delford 26, Valley Falls 13.

Chip looked at the clock. Twelve minutes to go and thirteen points behind. It was now or never. He looked anxiously toward the bench; there was no stirring about there. Rock wasn't going to use Speed. Chip knew then it was up to him. He'd use the spread . . . open up the playbook . . . try all Rock's strategies, even the bootleg play he had hoped to save for Steeltown.

Delford kicked directly to Chip. The home team was confident now. Chip carried to the thirty-four and immediately called the spread. Delford was caught by surprise. Before the Delford players had a chance to call a timeout and get organized, Chip passed to Schwartz for a gain of thirty-six yards. Then he tossed a nifty pass to Cody Collins, who was screened perfectly behind the shifted line. Collins scored without a hand touching him. Chip and Jordan Taylor teamed to score on another shaky point after. Delford 26, Valley Falls 20.

Delford received and the slight breeze that had suddenly sprung up carried Chip's high kick over the goal line for a touchback. The ball was brought out to the Delford twenty, and Chip called, "Time!"

A weary, played-out bunch gathered around Chip in the huddle. He glanced around at the players' tired faces. Rockwell had made only rare substitutions in the whole game.

"Listen, men," Chip said, "we've *got* to hold Delford now. Just *got* to! The spread has them on the run, but if we let them score again, it's all over. Look at the clock. Ten minutes to go. You guys keep them from scoring, and

I'll get you another touchdown and the extra point. What d'ya say?" He thrust out his hand, and they all joined in the team grip.

"We'll hold 'em!" Biggie vowed.

And hold them the Big Reds did. Delford was forced to kick from its twenty-three, and Chip took the ball on his forty-five at full speed. He bobbled the catch, but his juggling caused the charging ends to slow up a bit.

The little change of pace was precisely what Chip needed. His long legs stretched, and he broke between the converging ends and set out for the right sideline. He raced past midfield, the Delford forty-five, the forty, the thirty-five, all the way down to the twenty-eight before a mighty tackle by Pilsner knocked him out of bounds.

As the referee placed the ball on the nearer hash marks in from the sideline, Chip made up his mind to use the bootleg. It worked like magic. Chip faked a handoff to Chris Badger driving into the line, took three short steps toward Cody, and made a perfect fake to the chunky little halfback. Cody sprinted out to the other side of the field behind Robby Leonard and Soapy Smith, who had pulled out of the line. Collins had covered up perfectly, and after faking, Chip slowed down. And all the time he was holding the ball in his right hand behind his right hip.

The Delford left end never gave Chip a second look but pursued Collins instead. Then Chip turned on the steam. No need to fake any longer. He pulled the ball back under his arm and cut down the sideline.

He tightroped just inside the white-chalked line down the field toward the goal line. The Delford left half-back had shifted to the right when Leonard, Smith, and

BOOTLEG PLAY

Collins had swept in that direction. Now, too late, he discovered the ruse, turned, and made a futile dive at the speeding quarterback. Chip never slowed! He just ran and scored standing up. The Valley Falls rooters charged out on the field and ringed the sideline. Score: Valley Falls 26, Delford 26.

As Chip settled in for the place kick, he heard a long, rising crescendo ending with "Hilton. HILTON! HILTON!"

He carefully gauged the kick, swinging his leg once or twice to get his rhythm, and then began the count.

The ball came spiraling back from the three-yard line to Jordan, and Chip started his rocker. Taylor lost his focus and bobbled the ball. He was too anxious and the ball had slipped out of his hands. He recovered it quickly and placed it down, but it was too late. It seemed as if the whole Delford line broke through. The ball smacked against an outstretched hand and bounded back up the field with Chip in swift pursuit. The covering official immediately whistled to indicate the try and down were ended. The attempted kick had been blocked.

The Delford players' momentum carried them into Chip. They got up heavily and reluctantly. But Chip didn't care. Over and over he moaned, "At a time like this! At a time like this!"

It was the first kick he had missed all year.

CHAPTER 16

Double Safety

JORDAN "AIR" TAYLOR'S eyes filled with tears as the team gathered in the huddle behind the ball for the kick-off. "I lost the game," he managed, "I—I lost the game!"

Chip tapped him on the side of the helmet. "Cut it out," he growled. "I hurried you." He motioned the discouraged players closer around him. "Now, listen—"

As Chip backed up his seven steps behind the ball, he glanced at the clock. Seven minutes . . .

His eyes swept along the five Delford linemen who were positioned between the fifty-yard line and their own forty-five. Then he raised his arms to his side, held them there for a second, and started forward toward the ball.

"Watch out!" A heavy voice from the Delford bench bellowed. "Watch for an onside kick!"

The cry was immediately taken up by the players on the home bench, and just as Chip kicked the ball, the

DOUBLE SAFETY

Delford captain came running up the field. But he was too late. The ball went slithering and twisting along the ground and barely made it across the midfield stripe. It looked like a bad kick, but it wasn't. Chip had tried an onside kick.

Biggie Cohen drove straight for the ball as did two of the Delford linemen. When the three flying figures met, the crash was heard clear up in the stands. The Delford players had been alerted by the sideline clamor, but it was too late to react effectively. Air Taylor followed Biggie's mad rush and fell on the ball, clutching it with desperate hands and curling around it. It was Valley Falls's ball, first and ten, on Delford's forty-eight.

Chip grinned and called for the spread. A tie game was no good. *He* was playing to win.

The very first pass clicked. Delford was concentrating on Ted Williams and Red Schwartz, and Chip discovered Jordan Taylor in the left flat all alone. He gave the little halfback a short lead pass, and Jordan scampered down the left sideline for a twenty-six-yard gain. First down on the Delford twenty-two. The Delford captain called, "Time!"

Play resumed as the Big Reds again shifted into the spread, and Chip saw that four players were flanking Soapy and Trullo. They were going to blitz him.

As the ball came spiraling back, the four came charging toward him at full speed. Soapy and Trullo didn't have a chance to block them. Chip faded back nearly to the forty, all the time trying to find a free receiver. They were all covered. For a split second, he considered grounding the ball. But the risk was too great—the loss of a down and a fifteen-yard penalty.

He decided to run the ball and took off to the left. The momentum of the charging linemen was too much; they couldn't stop, and he turned them easily and got back up to the twenty-eight before he was downed. It was second down, sixteen yards for a first down. He looked at the clock again. There was plenty of time— nearly five minutes.

In the huddle he called for the flea-flicker from the spread. The first pitch was to go to Collins on the right side, followed by the flea-flicker lateral to Badger cutting behind Cody and toward the right sideline where the blockers were to form.

Chip faded back and slightly to the right. Collins came charging toward the left along the line of scrimmage, and Chip pegged a hard bullet pass right into Cody's waiting hands. Badger delayed and, a split second before Cody was tackled, cut behind him, took the lateral, and headed for the massed linemen near the right sideline. He nearly reached them. As he turned downfield, he slipped and one knee touched the ground. Chris staggered back to his feet, but the referee's whistle killed the play. The ball was dead where Chris's knee touched the ground.

Chip groaned. It was third and eighteen with the ball on Delford's thirty. Eighteen yards to go for a first down in two tries. From inside the huddle, he looked at the ground in front of the Delford goal. It was solid there and elevated just a bit.

"We've got to get in front of that goal so we can try a placement," he whispered. "I'll run it on a fake spinner with an end around. Give me some interference."

Chip spun out of his position behind Trullo and picked up Taylor, Badger, Smith, and Leonard for interference. He slid off Delford's right end and made the center of the field before he began to drive for the goal. He went down on the fifteen. Fourth down, now, and three yards to go for a first down. The ball was squarely in front of the Delford goal. Chip called, "Time!" He had to think this over.

On the sidelines, Speed Morris was talking excitedly to Coach Rockwell. "It's OK, Coach! You've *got* to send me in! I *belong* in there! See? My ankle's OK!" He jumped up and down and turned beseechingly to Pop Brown. Rockwell faced the little trainer.

Pop's eyes were imploring too. "He's all right, Coach," he said. "He couldn't turn that ankle with a wrench. There's yards of tape on it. See, the laces don't even meet!"

"All right," Rockwell said reluctantly. "Report for Taylor. Tell Chip to kick it!"

But Rockwell was talking to himself. Speed was on his way. He never heard the words. He joined a relieved Chip in the huddle.

"What'll we do?" Chip asked.

"What'll we do?" echoed Speed. "Why, we'll kick the ball clear over the bleachers. Three points are all we need now."

Trullo's snap couldn't have been better. Speed spotted the ball, and Chip drove his shoe through it with all his power. Then he focused directly at the spot where the ball had rested. He'd be sure to keep his head down on this one. Tug Watson would be pleased.

He never saw the ball sailing end over end, high and straight for the goal. The ball came down well behind the crossbar for the precious three points. Score: Valley Falls 29, Delford 26.

TOUCHDOWN PASS

The frantic Delford captain prepared to receive with three minutes left to play. Chip kicked to the Delford ten, and the runner was downed on the thirty. Chip knew what to expect now—so did everyone else. Time was running out. Delford would pass every time!

Chip called for a 5-3-3 defense. Delford went into its set formation and passed. It was a chance pass, but it clicked. Delford sent two receivers straight at Speed. Just as they reached him, they crossed. Speed covered one—the wrong one. Delford's lanky right end got behind him, reached up a long arm, hooked in the ball, and was on his way. Chip, taking the middle defensive spot, was forced to hold his position because Delford's left end outran Collins and headed right down the center of the field. But when the ball was in the air, Chip took off to help Speed.

Three strides too late, he headed diagonally down the field. He *had* to intercept the racing end this side of the goal line. This was one time he had to do the running all alone; Speed was out of it, and there wasn't anyone else on the squad who could match the speeding Delford player. Chip could hear chugging steps and labored breathing behind him but never looked back.

Inch by inch he gained. He'd have to dive at those flying heels soon. He made his try on the twenty, diving headlong, arms outstretched. One hand caught an ankle, and the big end crashed down on the fifteen-yard line. It was Delford's ball, first and ten on the Valley Falls fifteen with two minutes and five seconds left to play.

The Delford quarterback tried the line twice and then passed to the big right end again. Speed leaped but couldn't quite reach the ball and had to be satisfied with bringing the receiver down on the five-yard line. It was first and five yards for the winning touchdown.

DOUBLE SAFETY

Chip could have used a timeout now, but he had used his third and last for the half just before Speed entered the game. Coach Jinx Jenkins was jubilant! He wasn't going to settle for anything less than a touchdown. He was determined to beat Rockwell!

Delford discarded the huddle and used an established play series. There was no signal, merely the count for the snapping of the ball. But Valley Falls held firm. On fourth down with less than a foot to go, Biggie Cohen, Soapy Smith, and Nick Trullo all met the big Delford fullback at the line of scrimmage and flattened him. It was the Big Reds' ball, first and ten, on their own one-yard line with forty seconds to play.

"I'll kill the full twenty-five I'm allowed to put the ball in play," Chip whispered to the circle of tense faces.

"That's right," added Speed. "They can't hurt us by penalizing us. They can only penalize us half the distance to the goal line. That's about where we are now! Hang in there, guys!"

"Yeah," said Chip, "but don't forget that would stop the clock. Give me a good snap, Nick." There were twenty seconds to go as Chip started the count.

As Chip stood in the end zone, one yard away from the end line, he remembered something that almost made him laugh. It was Petey Jackson's tenth question, the one about the player who had scored for the other team.

The ball came back from Trullo, and the Delford line crashed through. Chip suddenly turned and ran parallel to the end line. If he could only hold that ball for a few more seconds! He didn't try to run the ball out of the end zone; he just tried to avoid the Delford players as long as possible.

TOUCHDOWN PASS

Time is running out all right, but they've got me boxed. Now I'll run out of bounds. Can't take the chance of being tackled and having them steal the ball.

He turned and ran across the end zone line and toward the bleachers at the end of the field. The referee's whistle shrilled, but that didn't save Chip from being tackled and hurled to the ground by the infuriated opponents. Even then, Chip held onto the ball, and the referee had to pry it out of his hands. "Smart play, kid," he muttered. "Smart play!"

The referee strode out in front of the goal and raised both arms over his head and placed the palms of his hands together. A safety.

The home stands roared, but their cheers fell away to a subdued babble of questions and wild explanations, as the scoreboard registered only two points for Delford. The score: Valley Falls 29, Delford 28.

"I can't believe it!" squealed Stan Gomez from the broadcasting booth. "Chip Hilton just scored for Delford! He ran around the end zone looking for a receiver—finding no one open. He finally took the ball over the end line resulting in a safety and two points for Delford. But it's OK as Valley Falls still leads by one point! One has to wonder about Coach Jenkins's decision to go for the touchdown a few moments ago instead of the field goal."

There were nine seconds to play when the referee placed the ball on the twenty-yard line. He motioned the Delford team to the thirty-yard line and cautioned both teams to stay behind their restraining lines until the ball had been kicked.

Chip advised the referee he would punt the ball. When his teammates gathered around him in the huddle, he whispered, "I'll kick it out of bounds near the fifty-yard line on the left side of the field. Everyone cover it. Remember, they'll have time for at least one play. They'll pass for sure. Stay in the 5-3-3 defense."

When the referee blew his whistle to start play, Chip booted the ball just as though he were practicing, and the ball spiraled across the sideline on the Big Reds' forty-six-yard line and bounced over the Delford bench.

Delford lined up in its regular formation. The big quarterback faded back, cocked his arm in the waning seconds, and threw a long pass down toward the right corner. It seemed as though every one of the Valley Falls defensive backs were there—Speed, Chip, Cody, and Chris. They all leaped in a knot of arms and bodies, and the ball went flying out of bounds. The game was over! Chip ran for the ball, but Speed beat him to it.

The Valley Falls players were all shouting as though they had won the state championship. The Delford managers pulled the ball out of Speed's hands. "I'll ask Coach Jenkins if you can have it," one said.

"That's our ball!" someone roared. Before the startled managers could move, Biggie Cohen almost lifted them from their feet as he wrenched the ball out of their arms and trotted to the dressing room.

It was several minutes before Rockwell could quiet the happy squad. "Boys," he said, "that was a great game! Chip's play was a double safety. A safety and two points for Delford, all right, but it was a game-saver for us. That was quick thinking and smart thinking, Chip."

A smile broke over his face as he nodded toward Burrell Rogers, standing quietly by the door with Dink Davis. "Mr. Rogers and I made a decision some time ago to take the whole squad to the Canton Inn, here in Delford, for dinner and afterward to a movie."

Every boy in the room cheered. Every boy except Chip Hilton. He had to get home. As Chip stood there dismayed, a strange hush fell over the room, and he followed everyone's eyes to the door, which seemed to be filled to overflowing by a heavy, red-faced, angry man.

"Where's the ball, Rockwell?" Jenkins demanded.

There was a short silence and then the belligerent Delford coach pounded the door with his fist. "I want that ball, and I want it now!"

"You mean the game ball?" Rockwell's voice was cool and composed.

"You know what ball I mean," Jenkins shouted, trembling with anger and frustration. "Where is it?"

Rockwell turned toward the boys. "If someone has it, I guess we'll have to give the young man his ball," he said softly. "He's going to have a stroke."

Biggie Cohen reached a big hand down in his bag and picked up the ball. Then he reluctantly handed it to Rockwell. "Coach, I wanted to give it to Chip," he said slowly. "He won the game!"

"You mean the officials won the game," sneered Jenkins. "The officials and that illegal formation you used all afternoon."

Rockwell tossed the ball carefully to the glowering coach. "You're a poor sport, Jenkins," he said coolly. "A poor sport in a lot of ways. You're sure welcome to the ball. None of my players would get a kick out of having that ball now. It would always remind them of a poor sport. Good-bye. Please close the door."

CHAPTER 17

The Best of Intentions

JINX JENKINS had been more successful in silencing the Big Reds in their own dressing room than his team had been on the field. The players dressed quietly. The display of poor sportsmanship they had just witnessed had taken something from their victory. The only irrepressible occupant of the dressing room was Soapy Smith. He was muttering,

There's a rat in Delford named Jenkins
Who's better known as Jinx
He can't meet your eye without blinkin'
And when he's around something stinks.

Chip lumbered over to Coach Rockwell's side. "Coach," he began hesitantly, "I'd like to pass up the dinner if it would be all right with you. We're having something special at home tonight, and—and I really do have to be there. Somehow, I've got to be there by seven o'clock."

TOUCHDOWN PASS

Rockwell had been quiet and deep in thought since Jenkins's locker room temper tantrum, and the eyes he turned toward Hilton still wore a depressed look. He studied Chip for a moment, and then his eyes warmed with a kindly light.

"Why, I guess it will be all right, Chip, if your mom knows. There's a bus out of here every hour or so. You go ahead, Chipper. Do you have enough money?"

But Rockwell had been mistaken. Chip had just missed the five o'clock bus. The next one left at seven o'clock, and he was supposed to meet Mr. Browning at the Sugar Bowl at seven.

A dejected Chip Hilton stood on the sidewalk, debating what to do next. With a screech of brakes and a blast from a horn, a shiny red MG sports car slid to a stop right in front of him.

"Hey, Chip! You look like part of the losing team rather than one of the winners. Where's the team?"

Chip hesitated, "Team's gone out for a victory dinner. I'm supposed to be home by seven o'clock, and I just missed the bus."

"Sounds important! Come on. Hop in! Tell old man Thomas all about it." Brandon Thomas leaned over the gear shift and opened the door of the car.

"Thanks, Brandon, but I'll be OK. Told Coach I was going to take the bus."

"Is that all? Forget it! Hop in. I'll have you there by six!"

Chip was in a quandary. Rockwell thought he was going home by bus, and everyone knew how the Rock felt about players riding in cars. But wasn't this different? Rock meant high school kids. Brandon was older, more mature, a college student.

THE BEST OF INTENTIONS

"Come on, come on," urged Thomas. "What's the big deal? I'll have you home before you know it. Besides, I'm in a hurry myself, and I could use the company!" Brandon swung the car door wide and sat upright behind the wheel.

Chip shook his head indecisively, then dropped into the seat, and closed the door. A squeal of rubber, a grinding of gears, and they were on their way.

Brandon Thomas hadn't been bragging, Chip was thinking; at this rate they *would* be home before six o'clock. He glanced at the speedometer again. It registered seventy-five.

He started to remind Brandon to slow down, but it was nearing dusk and the two-lane road was tricky. Brandon was focused at the wheel, engrossed in his driving, and Chip decided to wait until they reached a straight stretch before saying anything.

A little later, he breathed a sigh of relief. Brandon was slowing down. Chip didn't see the roadside inn until the sleek sports car slid to a stop with protesting brakes. Brandon turned to Chip and grinned. "I need a little liquid refresher! How about you?"

Chip shook his head. "Not me, thanks. I'll wait."

He waited all right. Nearly half an hour passed. He got out of the car, walked past the humming neon signs in the window, and opened the inn's door. Music was blaring, and four or five laughing people were gathered around a noisy video game. No one even noticed his entrance. Brandon and a group of men were sitting around a smoky table, talking excitedly. Several bottles and a number of glasses were on the table. Chip figured Brandon was rehashing the game. He tried to get his attention, but it was no use. Brandon was gesturing and moving his head, holding the interest of everyone at the table.

"Forget this!" Chip muttered. He decided to start walking. Maybe someone would be going home from the game and would pick him up.

It was nearly dark now. Although several cars passed by, none stopped. Chip kept moving, thinking all the while about the game and the players. They were probably eating dinner right now, and Soapy would be adding numerous verses and embellishments to his Jinx Jenkins poem.

He had felt bad about leaving, but at least Biggie and Speed knew why he was in such a hurry to get home. The whole group had cheered him, and Speed had said, "Beat it, champ! I'll bring your stuff! You just save me some of that cake."

A few minutes later, he heard a car slowing, and Brandon skidded to a stop. "Sorry, Chip. Got talking to some guys about the game." Chip glanced sideways at the carefree college student. Brandon seemed to be in a happy mood. Maybe too happy . . .

Brandon Thomas came from an affluent Valley Falls family but never made a pretense of being anything other than what he was—an easygoing guy. Unlike Joel Ohlsen, Brandon never mentioned his family, his money, or any of the advantages he enjoyed. Chip had always liked that about Brandon, although they knew each other only casually.

"You can take it easy, Brandon," Chip said as the seat belt clicked. "I've got lots of time now."

Brandon responded by pressing even harder on the gas pedal. "Don't worry, Chip," he said, "I could drive this road blindfolded." The car sailed around the sharp curves. Then it happened!

THE BEST OF INTENTIONS

A tractor-trailer was parked on the roadside, and a station wagon, at first concealed by the deep curve in the road, was creeping along now directly in front of Brandon.

Chip gripped the side of the door and looked for an opening. He shot toward the dashboard as Brandon jammed on the brakes. The car swerved dangerously. Chip braced his feet and pushed back against his seat. For one wild, fleeting moment it looked as though Brandon had lost his head completely and would smash directly into the back of the parked rig.

At the last second, he veered to the left and tried to pass the station wagon using the oncoming lane. Brandon oversteered. The sports car's left wheels dropped dangerously onto the narrow gravel shoulder.

Chip caught a blur of the horrified faces of the people in the station wagon. Brandon was fighting desperately with the wheel and trying to get control. For an instant, Chip thought they'd made it.

In a brief moment of unreality, trees, fences, hills, and road careened before Chip's eyes and then—darkness. The brittle sound of breaking glass softened into the whir, whir, whirring of the tires, which continued to spin in contact with nothing but the air, and then all was silent.

Something tremendously heavy was lying across Chip's face, and as he struggled to push it away, he heard voices as if from a great distance.

"He's coming to now," someone said.

Coming to? Chip struggled to a sitting position and tried to stand up. But someone was holding his arms. Gradually the room stopped spinning, and, as his eyes focused, Chip wiped cold sweat from his forehead and gazed around the room in astonishment.

"What is this? Where am I?"

Doc Jones smiled slightly. "This is a hospital, and you're in it! But stop your yelling. You'll wake everybody up. It's ten o'clock."

"Ten o'clock!" Chip again tried to rise. "Hey, I've got to get . . . Hey, what's wrong with my leg?" He felt along a cast and bandages. "I must be having a nightmare!"

"A nightmare is right!" Doc Jones agreed. "How do you feel?"

Chip felt his head and looked at the cuts on his hands. "OK, I guess." He sank back on the pillow. Everything came back to him . . . the wild ride . . . the wreck . . . the semi . . . the station wagon . . .

"Doc," he whispered, "where's Brandon? How did I get here? What about my leg?"

"It's broken, Chip," Jones said quietly. He placed his fingers on Chip's wrist and felt his pulse. "But otherwise, you're all right."

"But otherwise, you're all right." Chip repeated, turning his head away and meeting the remorseful eyes of Brandon Thomas lying in the next bed.

"I'm sorry, Chip," Brandon grimaced. "I'm really sorry. Guess there's not much else I can say."

Chip raised himself on his elbows. "I—"

Jones placed a firm hand on his shoulder. "Now, Chip. You'll have to lie quietly. There's nothing you can do that hasn't been done, and nothing for you to worry about."

"But Mom and—and Mr. Browning—"

"Everything's been taken care of," Jones said, placing a hand on Chip's forehead. "Everything went as you planned. When I got you up here in the hospital, I called your mother, and she came right up. Petey Jackson and

THE BEST OF INTENTIONS

George Browning came too. They stayed here until I sent them home and told them to go ahead with the party. Mr. Browning was as stubborn as a mule, and I had to push him out of the room. Your mother finally got him to go. She's been here all evening. Since you're awake, I'll have a nurse bring her in." He smiled and nodded his head. "They'll all be back here in the morning. Now you rest, and I'll be around tomorrow to check on you."

"But, Doc, my leg—is it bad?"

"You're a lucky kid, Chip. You've got an injury at the lower end of the fibula and tibia, probably caused by a violent wrench of the ankle." Noting Chip's bewildered expression, he explained, "It's not really as bad as it sounds, thank goodness. You've got a fractured ankle. I was more worried about the fact you were unconscious than I was about the leg. It'll be all right. All an injury of that kind needs is rest and immobility."

Jones chuckled at Chip's expression. "It's not bad. You'll be up on crutches in a few days and out of here soon."

"Crutches! No way! Doc, you mean I won't be able to play in the Rutledge game—not even in the Steeltown game? Hey! Nothing doing! I gotta play—"

"Now look, Chip. Get it through your head right now! You won't be able to play any more football this year, and you'll not be able to play any basketball either, for a couple of months at least."

Chip gazed into the doctor's eyes for a long second, breathed a deep sigh of anguish, and once again fell back on the pillow.

Jones looked at the athlete's pale, worried face and then patted Chip's shoulder reassuringly. "One season doesn't make a career, Chip. A winner always keeps his chin up and takes the bad with the good. See you tomorrow, champ!"

Chip had never been confined to a hospital. Saturday night he hadn't slept. Neither had Brandon Thomas. Brandon had been as nervous and worried as Chip.

"I'm a dead man when I get home," Brandon moaned. "I almost wish my leg was broken. Imagine! They can't find a thing wrong with me—just keepin' me here for observation. They better observe me after I get home! Dad's going to be all over me. Guess I've seen my first and last sports car for a while!"

Chip had little opportunity to be lonesome. On Sunday, he had one visitor after another. Mary Hilton stayed all day, only visiting the cafeteria to make room for other visitors. George Browning, Mrs. Browning, Taps, and Suzy came and left.

Chip's teammates and friends began to appear. First came Speed, Biggie, and Soapy. Then Petey Jackson arrived with a big bunch of roses from Mr. Schroeder and two boxes of candy for Chip's nurses. Petey and Soapy kept everyone in stitches with their wisecracks. Soapy ate most of the candy and told the nurses the flowers were really from him.

After a rest in the afternoon, it was more visitors— Ted Williams, Lou Mazotta, Robby Leonard, Jordan Taylor, and even the South Side crew—Chris Badger, Cody Collins, and Nick Trullo.

J. P. Ohlsen called Chip to thank him for his courage and his part in apprehending Bracken, the guilty caster. He also said to heal fast and not to worry about hospital expenses because they were covered by the pottery's insurance plan.

THE BEST OF INTENTIONS

Brandon Thomas's father took his son home Sunday morning and told Chip the car and its occupants were completely insured. There would be no need for Mr. Ohlsen's insurance. Brandon's eyes conveyed a message of regret at leaving. Chip gripped Brandon's hand firmly.

"Everything's OK, Brandon. See you later!"

On Monday Doc Jones released Chip from the hospital after examining the plaster cast. "From now on," Jones said, "it's only a matter of time. Before you know it, you'll be barging around again under your own power."

Chip was elated to be going home. He figured the crutches were a necessary evil. But, if they would get him home, he could stand them.

"Remember," Doc Jones warned, "weight-bearing must be controlled. You'll be putting a little weight on it each day, and that's all right, but no trying to play football with those crutches! If you behave yourself and follow instructions, maybe you can go to a game soon."

Saturday, November 18, was an open date on the Big Reds' schedule. Practically every player on the team joined Chip in his living room by the radio. Coach Rockwell had taken Speed, Biggie Cohen, and Ted Williams to scout Rutledge.

Coach Rockwell visited Chip three times over the next few days. Chip tried to find a way to explain the reason for the trip home in the car, but the words just didn't seem to come. Rockwell was sympathetic and repeated Doc Jones's assurances that the leg would heal "stronger than ever." Rockwell told Chip about the shifts that he needed to make on the team. He was using Soapy Smith at left halfback and had moved Speed to quarterback. Speed demonstrated he could throw a short pass fairly well. Rockwell was planning to let Speed run a lot from the new position. "Don't worry about a thing, Chip," Rockwell said. "Next year, we'll have another veteran team, and it'll be *our* turn!"

After Rockwell's last visit, Chip felt depressed. He was sure Rock thought he had lied about the trip home. Sometimes the best of intentions . . .well . . . anyway . . . The Brownings were together again . . . Mr. Browning had his job back . . . Taps wouldn't be moving and could go out for the basketball team.

Whenever Chip looked down at the cast on his leg, his thoughts grew bitter. Doc Jones said the leg would be all right if there were no complications. But what if there were complications? What if he could never play football again . . . or basketball . . . or baseball?

The following Saturday, Valley Falls defeated Rutledge. Soapy Smith was both the hero and the goat. After running the wrong way on a lateral-pass play, Soapy made up for everything by intercepting a Rutledge pass and running it back for a touchdown and the winning points. On the wrong-way run, Soapy would have scored for Rutledge if Speed had not tackled him on the Valley Falls twenty-yard line. The final score of the game was Valley Falls 13, Rutledge 7. Chris Badger had burst through the line for the other touchdown.

On Wednesday afternoon Speed came to Chip's house right after practice. He told Chip about the practice that day and the preparations Rockwell was making for Steeltown and Charles Minor, its great veteran back. Then the conversation lagged.

Chip sensed something was puzzling Speed. "Well?" he said.

THE BEST OF INTENTIONS

Speed cleared his throat. "Chip," he hesitated, then went on, "what's the matter with you and the Rock? Why do you act so funny when he comes to see you?"

"I don't know, Speed. I don't know how to start—"

"Start what?"

"Explaining about the accident, that's what!"

"Just tell him the truth. Just tell him what happened—that Brandon Thomas coaxed you to ride home with him and you never left the car except to start walking home."

"I can't do that. Anyway, he never gives me a chance—just keeps talking all the time he's near me."

"Look, Chip," Speed began, "the Rock just wants you to know he understands, and if you talk to him, it will be OK. You know he's responsible for all players on trips. He never lets anyone come home after a game in a car unless it's with his family. He doesn't even like it then. But, the way things stand now, people think he let you come home in Brandon's car, and that makes it look like you got special treatment. You know the Rock isn't like that."

"I know, Speed. I know I shouldn't have gone, but it's done. What do you want me to do?"

"Quit feeling sorry for yourself, for one thing, and tell Coach the whole story, for another. That's what! He's probably blaming himself for what happened to you."

Chip said nothing. Speed just didn't understand. How could he tell the Coach about the missed bus, that he hadn't planned to come back in a car, that Brandon had coaxed him? He couldn't blame Brandon; he didn't *have* to come back in the car. It all just sounded like a bunch of excuses.

CHAPTER 18

Grandstand Quarterback

ON FRIDAY night, it seemed that Rockwell had called a practice for the entire team at the Hilton home. First, it was Taps. He had been observing the afternoon's workout along with about every other loyal fan in Valley Falls and bubbled with news of the team. Later, Speed, Biggie, Soapy, Ted Williams, and Red Schwartz dropped in, and this group was enlarged a few minutes later by Jordan Taylor, Chris Badger, Cody Collins, and Lou Mazotta.

Soapy, as usual, took charge. He began to question the guys about the answers to Petey Jackson's final football quiz. "Fats Ohlsen has been complainin' all week about someone lettin' the air out of his tires at the Waterbury game," Soapy announced. "Now, come on—who done it?"

"Did it," Biggie corrected.

"Done it!" Soapy retorted obstinately. "Do! Done! Did! Do is any old tense, but did is past! Been there. Done that!" He looked around for support. "See, it can't be past tense until we know who done it!" He grinned widely, shrugged his shoulders, and looked around at the resigned faces. "OK, huh?"

Red Schwartz groaned. Soapy frowned at Red, then continued, "Well, I've got my own deductions to that one. Wanna know my answers?" He proudly pulled a piece of paper from his pocket. "This is a copy of the answers I turned in. Boy, I can taste those chocolates right now!"

He read aloud: "Number One: 'Who let the air out of Fats Ohlsen's tires at the Waterbury game?'" Soapy looked around triumphantly. "Petey Jackson himself!"

"Aw, everybody knows that," Badger said.

"Yeah? Fats doesn't!" Soapy snickered. "Number Two: 'Where was Coach Rockwell between halves of the November 4 game?' Duh! That's easy! Gettin' Valley Falls's biggest dork out of a jam!

"Number Three: 'What great football authority provided the questions and answers for the previous quizzes?' That's a no-brainer! The only guy in town who knows 'em all—the Rock!

"Number Four: 'What transpired in Coach Rockwell's office when three prominent South Side athletes were called on the carpet?'" Soapy cautiously eyed Badger and Collins, and then continued with a sickly smile.

"The Rock—" He floundered and looked for help. But there was no help, and he stumbled on. "The Rock, um, the Rock asked them why they didn't move to the West Side!" Soapy breathed a sigh of relief and looked around the quiet group. "Clever, eh?"

There was no response. Soapy shrugged his shoulders and continued.

"Number Five: 'What happened when the "Battle of the Locker Room" was discussed in Mr. Zimmerman's office?' That's easy! Zimmerman asked Pop Brown who won the decision.

"Number Six: 'What Chip Hilton protégé may create history on the Valley Falls hardcourt?' That's too easy—Taps Browning!

"Number Seven: 'What player disregarded Coach Rockwell's orders and saved Valley Falls from defeat?' Everyone knows that one. Gentlemen, I give you the one and only—Chip Hilton! He passed the ball to Speed Morris on fourth down in the Hampton game instead of kicking, and Morris ran for a touchdown to tie the score and save the team from defeat!

"Number Eight: 'Who calls Speed Morris every Sunday morning and for what reason?' Only one guy would have enough nerve to call Speed Morris! Chip Hilton's gray eyes turn green every Sunday morning because he gets up at eight o'clock for church while Speed Morris can sleep until noon if he wants to. So, Hilton calls the Morris domicile to arouse his pal—those two share everything—misery and joy!"

"It's domicile, you imbecile," Red Schwartz cracked, "not 'domicile'!"

Soapy ignored him.

"Number Nine: 'How old is Pop Brown? How long has he been trainer at Valley Falls? What did he do before coming to Valley Falls?'

"Pop Brown is an oxygenarian—"

Everyone in the room howled. Red Schwartz finally managed, "Octogenarian, clown, octogenarian!"

Soapy regarded his laughing teammates haughtily. "A guy can make a mistake once in a while, can't he?

GRANDSTAND QUARTERBACK

"Pop Brown is an—Pop Brown is more than eighty years of age, and he's been at Valley Falls for more than thirty-seven years. He used to train pugilists. Prize fighters to you, Schwartz!

"Finally, Number Ten! 'What prominent person in Valley Falls once won a game for the Big Reds by scoring for the other team?'

"This answer will dazzle you! Before the great Hilton was born, J. P. Ohlsen, playing for Valley Falls High, scored a safety for the other team and saved the Big Reds from defeat." Soapy breathed a deep sigh of satisfaction and concluded with, "End quote!"

"About time!" Schwartz growled.

"Well, guys," Biggie Cohen said quietly, "this time tomorrow night we'll be state champions or just another team." Everyone's face sobered.

"We'll be state champs!" Soapy was emphatic.

"Not unless we can stop Minor," Ted Williams reminded the suddenly serious group.

"You know all the plays, Soapy?" Chip asked the red-faced comedian.

"Yeah, yeah, I guess so—all but the bootleg."

"I don't know that too well either, Chip," Speed said. "You better explain it to both of us. Here, put it on this piece of paper and then Soapy and I can walk through it."

Chip carefully drew the play, explaining that the heavy line was the path of the ball.

TOUCHDOWN PASS

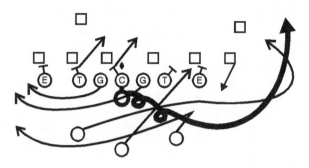

"You've got to set it up by running a few reverses first, Speed," Chip cautioned, "until you find one of the other team's ends who tries to angle after the halfback and tackle him from behind. The way it's set up here—to the right. Soapy's in motion out to the right before the ball is passed. Speed, you fake to the fullback, just as you do on the regular reverse, then fake to the halfback, and continue on around the end with the ball.

"If you fake your passing well, keep the ball out of sight, and slow up, keep cool, and act nonchalant—well, half the battle's won. You've got to hold the ball behind you with one hand and half-fake to cover the ball with the hand and arm nearest to the defensive end. If you dip your left or inside shoulder, it helps. When you get by the end, you're on your own. In reality, after you get up to the line, it's just like running in the open field, and everyone knows there isn't anyone any better than you in that category!"

At nine o'clock the telephone rang. Speed answered.

"Hello? Yes. This is Speed Morris. Sure, Petey. He did? Good! He's right here. Wait, I'll tell him." Speed turned to Soapy.

GRANDSTAND QUARTERBACK

"You won the prize! What d'ya know?" A faint smile spread over his lips. "Well! What are you waitin' for?" He turned back to the phone. "Bring it right over. Hurry up! You'll bring it yourself? Good!" Speed turned back to the group with a satisfied smile.

"Petey's bringing the prize right now—a five-pound box of candy. Anybody hungry?"

Soapy was on his feet. "Nothin' doin'! Nothin' doin'! I got a plan for those chocolates, and it don't include no football players!"

"No?" Biggie Cohen reached out a big paw and pulled Soapy down on the couch beside him. "Now, Soapy," he said, "you know we're a team—one for all and all for one! Besides, who you thinkin' about givin' them to anyway?"

At nine-thirty, a group of Valley Falls football players and one happy Sugar Bowl manager smacked their lips appreciatively and glanced regretfully at an empty box and all the empty wrappers that had covered Soapy's chocolates. Soapy wasn't as bothered as he pretended to be. Nothing kept Soapy Smith down very long.

Chip was sorry to see them leave, but he knew they were all thinking about the game and wanted to get to bed early. "Good luck, guys," he called, "if I don't see you before the game."

"We'll kill 'em!" Soapy shouted back.

Chip was up early the next morning, scanning the sky with anxious eyes from his bedroom window. Later, he hobbled out on the back porch where he studied the clear, bright sky and thrilled to the feel of the crisp, early morning air.

TOUCHDOWN PASS

All morning he sat at the living room window, watching people hurry along the street. Many waved to him, and a few neighbors dropped in for a short visit to ask how he was feeling. Just before noon, Chip was surprised to see Coach Rockwell's car stop in front of the gate. Rockwell came hurrying up the walk, waved to Chip, and made his way directly to the living room.

"Only have a second, Chipper! Could sure use you out on that field today, but I'm making you a sort of assistant coach instead. A sort of grandstand quarterback. Speed will pick you up and bring you to the field early. We've all got to pitch in if we're going to win this one!"

He gripped Chip's shoulder tightly, and his voice was brittle.

"You've got to help, kiddo. You know all our plans and you know Steeltown. Watch their defense! That's where they're strong. I think we can hold Minor, but we've got to have a scoring play. That's where you can help! You're going to sit up in the grandstand, Chipper, just as we did at Steeltown, and look for things we can't see down on the sidelines.

"You know our plays better than anyone else, and you'll be able to see the weaknesses in Steeltown's defense and the plays that will work. I'm counting on you, Chip!

"Speed tells me Taps Browning will sit up there with you and be your runner. Now, don't hesitate a second to send him down to the bench with any tips you have. It's too bad we don't have a scouting box up there with a field phone down to the bench. We'll have one next year—you can be sure of that—one for the visiting team too!"

All roads led to Ohlsen Stadium that day. Before noon, cars were lined up for blocks on their way to the stadium parking lot. Steeltown and Valley Falls pennants and novelty footballs were on sale at every corner. Even the police on special duty seemed to have caught the spirit of the day.

Chip wanted to see the early warm-up practice of both teams. After Speed dropped Taps and him off at the gate, Chip followed his tall friend toward the end zone behind the north goal. As he followed Taps with slow, clumsy progress up the aisle to the last row of concrete seats, he was greeted on every side.

Joel Ohlsen saw him coming and shook his head with mock sympathy. "All Hail! Let's welcome the wannabe hero, Wheels," he jeered. "The grandstander has found his proper place at last—in the bleachers!"

Chip disregarded Ohlsen completely. Joel's sharp digs couldn't touch him anymore. J. P.'s phone call to Chip in the hospital had created a bond of friendship Joel's sarcasm could not break. Chip felt great knowing Mr. Ohlsen was his friend.

He paused to rest and looked down at the field. He'd give anything to be down there this afternoon. He continued his slow progress. Taps made no effort to help him. That was one of the many qualities making Taps such a good friend—understanding a guy's pride and his need for self-reliance.

CHAPTER 19

Old Forty-Four

CHIP HILTON, co-captain of the Valley Falls High School football team, was sitting in the bleachers for the first time in his high school life. The fact struck home and brought feelings of guilt. He'd let the school and the team down. But the thought was fleeting. He was soon engrossed in the action on the field.

Steeltown had controlled the game during the first half. Charles Minor, the big senior veteran, ran wild to score two touchdowns. At the half, the Steelers led 12–0.

In the first two periods, Chip looked for some way to help the Big Red offense or defense but saw nothing. Steeltown was too big, too strong in the line. He tried to put himself in Coach Rockwell's place. What would the Rock have looked for? He'd have looked for a weakness, some flaw or clue that might permit the use of a trick play.

But trick plays were no good. Good, solid preparation was what the doctor ordered; the right game situation would enable the Rock to use the strategies he held in reserve. Chip looked for a situation, but without success.

He limped slowly down the bleachers and along the sidelines to the bench. There he sandwiched himself between Taps and Miguel and remained there. He'd seen all there was to see from the stands: a big nothing!

The Big Reds were playing a magnificent defensive game. Outkicked and outgained, they tightened up in the shadow of their own goal time after time to stop Minor cold and to take over the ball on downs.

In the third quarter, Biggie blocked one of Minor's punts. The big tackle took the ball right off the star's shoe, and Valley Falls had the ball on the Steelers' thirty-yard line, first and ten. Speed fed Badger a quick handoff through the center of the line for three yards and then used Cody Collins on the first play of Rock's bootleg series. Collins made two yards—third down and five to go.

Chip's heart was pounding. Steeltown had scouted the Delford game and must have seen the plays Valley Falls had used to set up the bootleg. The Steelers must have seen him run the bootleg for the touchdown that tied up the Delford game at 26–all. Maybe they wouldn't remember the series plays though.

He nudged Taps. "Here it comes," he said. "Everything's set up perfectly. Watch Steeltown's left end—he's angling in to follow Cody around on the reverse."

Speed handled the ball with dexterity. After faking to Badger and Collins, he sped around right end and scored without a Steeltown player coming near enough for a tackle. It was a twenty-five-yard run. The score: Steeltown 12, Valley Falls 6.

Chip could guess what Speed was thinking in the huddle—how to make that extra point. But the decision wasn't left up to Speed. Rockwell sent Jordan Taylor in to replace Soapy Smith and to tell Speed to try a fake place kick. Speed did just that.

Taylor kneeled down as he had done for Chip and feigned preparations for a place kick. Speed lined up the attempt. But that was as close as it came to being a place kick. Trullo snapped the ball directly to Speed. He tried to get around right end. But the field had softened up, and he hadn't been able to get a fast start. Steeltown didn't fall for the deception. The Steelers knew Speed had never place-kicked for the Big Reds and had anticipated a run or a pass. Speed was downed on the one-yard line. The score remained unchanged.

Biggie Cohen kicked off and, following the ball, dumped the runner on the Steelers' twenty-yard stripe with a solid, vicious tackle. Steeltown took a timeout. Chip watched his red-clad teammates intently. They were grouped together ten yards ahead of the ball. A short distance away the Steelers stood in a circle.

Chip could see Speed, Ted, Chris, Jordan, and Biggie talking excitedly. Biggie pointed toward the scoreboard and then the ball that separated the two teams. Chip figured Biggie was saying, "We've gotta get that ball!" Yes, the Big Reds sure did have to get that ball.

Biggie towered above Speed and even Ted Williams, but he didn't look very big compared to Steeltown. The Iron Men were bigger all right—on the line, in the backfield, and, more importantly, on the scoreboard. Chip instinctively moved closer to Taps, who was tensely silent, peering over hand-clasped knees at the players on the field.

The chill of the late afternoon shadows closed in on the big stadium and drove the Valley Falls supporters

OLD FORTY-FOUR

into a shell. No longer was their cheering a thunder of precision and confidence. Despite the pleading of Dink Davis and the cheerleaders, only scattered and disorganized shouts of encouragement from a few die-hards could be heard. Even they seemed resigned to the inevitable.

Across the field it was different. A steady chant of exultation rang out from the happy fans behind the Steeltown bench.

Chip wasn't cold. He felt nothing but the hopelessness of a situation he could do nothing about. Over and over he repeated the Rock's favorite slogan: "A game is never lost until the final whistle." Nevertheless, there wasn't much hope in his worried eyes as he turned toward the scoreboard. Time was running out, and Valley Falls was still six points behind. Those six points loomed larger and larger with each passing second.

With three minutes left to play, it was Steeltown's ball, on its own twenty-yard line. The Iron Men were deliberate in their actions. When play resumed, the Steeltown quarterback tried to use up every possible second, slowing down the plays, killing time in the huddle, and holding the ball as long as possible. He wasn't risking a fumble either. Every play was a time-consuming quarterback sneak with little or no effort being made to advance the ball.

Chip's teammates were charging through the big Steeltown line as if it were paper, and Biggie Cohen was trying desperately to steal the ball. The game was nearly over, but in spite of Steeltown's stalling strategy and attempts to beat the clock, there were forty-five seconds to play and six yards to go when fourth down was called.

Would the Iron Men keep the ball for another running play or would they kick? Chip mentally debated the situation. If they attempted one more running or passing play and failed to make the necessary yardage for first down, Valley Falls would be awarded the ball and would have time left for a possible touchdown pass. It was a difficult decision to make.

The seconds ticked away as the Steeltown quarterback held his team in the huddle. He meant to use up every one of the precious seconds he was allowed to put the ball in play. He watched the official intently. He knew the penalty for delaying the game—five yards—and the clock would be stopped until the center snapped the ball. He wasn't going to risk that.

Just as the official started forward to warn the Steeltown captain, the Iron Men left the huddle and moved slowly up to the line. On the quarterback's signal, they shifted into kick formation.

The big linemen dug in their cleats, determined to hold their charging opponents. The Steelers couldn't afford to have *this* kick blocked.

Only seconds remained now, and Speed was running back to midfield to wait for the kick.

Chip and Taps braced their shoulders together.

"Speed might do it!"

The Steeltown ends were off with the snap of the ball. They drove straight down the field until they heard the thump of shoe on leather and then converged on Speed.

Morris, standing on the Big Reds' forty-five-yard line, gazed almost directly over his head, arms extended, hands ready to grasp the ball.

The Valley Falls fans gaped in amazement—Morris had evidently lost the ball in the gathering darkness. But how could that be? Anyone could see that the kick had been partially blocked and the ball was going to fall far ahead of Speed. They began to scream—to point toward the ball—to gaze at one another in amazed disbelief.

As the spinning ball nosed downward, Speed leaned forward and streaked upfield to the ball. The Steeltown ends were completely fooled by Speed's "lost ball" ruse, and, before they could change direction, he was yards up the field where he made a shoestring catch of the ball on a dead run.

Swift and straight, he sped until he was almost to the line of scrimmage. Then he reversed his field and drove along the sideline only seconds away from a touchdown. Speed had brought the ball up the field so fast the big Steeltown players never did get into the play.

Only Minor was between Speed and the goal. He was a sure tackler. He was shrewd too. He forced Speed toward the sideline and then broke the heart of every Falls faithful with a bone-crushing tackle that sent Speed spinning out of bounds.

Chip looked at the clock. The ball was dead when it went out of bounds, and the clock stopped. There were five seconds left to play, but time would not start until the ball was snapped by the center. Speed was still on the ground just out of bounds; he was taking advantage of the brief respite on the stopped clock. Chip's mind was working madly. This was what the Rock meant by the right strategic situation. . . .

What would Steeltown expect with only five seconds left to play? Why a pass, of course . . . or a run by Speed Morris. What would Chip do if he were calling the signals now? He'd pass, but Speed couldn't pass. Why not a fake pass? Why not the old Statue of Liberty play? At the Hilton A.C., he said Speed called it "old forty-four." It was stale and almost as old as the forward pass, yet the play always seemed to pop up in unexpected games. That was it! Old forty-four.

He grabbed a startled Soapy. "You know forty-four, Soapy? Well, listen! You've got to run it. Speed'll fake a pass, and you delay. Then cut behind him from the left halfback position, take the ball off his hand, and run wide around right end as you never ran before!"

Pulling the sputtering Soapy along behind him, he grasped Coach Rockwell by the arm. "Forty-four will do it, Coach," he insisted. "Soapy's seen Speed and me practice it a thousand times! He can do it! Speed can fake the pass, and Soapy can run the ball!"

Rockwell never hesitated. "You're right, Chip. It's perfect. Soapy, take Taylor's place! Tell Speed to use forty-four!"

Chip watched Speed with a pounding heart. Maybe Speed was hurt . . . wouldn't be able to finish . . .

In the broadcasting booth, Stan Gomez, exhausted from the excitement of Speed's run, declared, "It was a great run, folks. Speed Morris nearly made it—nearly— but not quite. With seconds to go Morris ran a Steeltown punt from his own forty-five down to the Steeler twelve.

"There's only five seconds left in this game. Time is out because Minor spilled Morris out of bounds on that tackle. Well, Valley Falls—or I'd better say Speed Morris, if he gets up—still has another chance to tie this game. It's a slim chance but still a chance. Morris is up now.

"Here comes a Big Red substitution. It's Smith, number 66, and he's replacing Taylor at left half. Valley Falls breaks from the huddle. They're coming up to the line. There's the snap—Morris is back—he's going to pass— he's looking for a receiver—no one is open—looks like he's being rushed by the whole Steeltown line.

OLD FORTY-FOUR

"They're going to hit him—he hasn't moved—he *fumbles!* No—no—Smith took the ball out of Morris's hand from the rear, and he's cutting around this side of the field. He's coming out here all alone—the Steeltown secondary is chasing him now—Minor is going to cut him down—no—Minor just got a hand on him. Smith stumbled, but he's still on his feet—he's staggering now. Here comes Biggie Cohen, Smith is on the five—an Iron Man hits him—Biggie Cohen blocks the Steeltown tackler—they're all falling—Smith is—over! YES—SMITH SCORES—SMITH SCORES!"

Chip was trying to yell, but no sound came. Perhaps, though, it was because another voice more or less wouldn't have been heard anyway; the stadium was one steady roar of sound that smothered even the ability to think.

Chip hopped up and down on one foot, looking up at the scoreboard. Valley Falls 12, Steeltown 12. There was no more time on the clock, but the game wasn't over. The Big Reds had a chance to win the mythical state title by scoring the point after touchdown. Once again, Chip's mind was racing.

The Rock never liked the drop kick, but he didn't know how much of an expert Speed was with this weapon. Chip glanced fearfully at the turf in front of the goal. It was soggy, maybe muddy was the correct word, but Speed could do it. He *knew* Speed could do it.

Once again, Chip grasped Rockwell by the arm.

"Please, Coach," he pleaded, "please let Speed dropkick. He's deadly on the short ones!"

Rockwell's black eyes darted from Chip out to the field and back again. "Look at the ground, Chip," he directed. "The ground is bad. It's a stretch."

TOUCHDOWN PASS

He turned and roared for Jordan Taylor. "Go in for Smith. Tell Morris to drop-kick!" He shook the little back's shoulders until the helmet, which Taylor had never fastened, slid down over his eyes.

"Let's do it! Make it happen!" Rockwell shouted. "Tell Morris to drop-kick it himself!" He half-pushed, half-propelled Taylor across the sideline. "Hurry!" he yelled.

Chip could scarcely breathe. Speed could do it! He looked down at the cumbersome cast on his leg. All the hours he had spent developing his kicking . . . wasted . . . just when he was needed most. Why did he have to be the one to get hurt? Why couldn't it have been Brandon Thomas? Brandon didn't even play football, and Brandon didn't have to work either. Suddenly ashamed of his thoughts, Chip looked out on the field again. Well, he didn't really mean it that way. . . .

The stadium was quiet now except for a determined "Block that kick! Block that kick!" roaring across the field from behind the Steeltown bench.

Speed dropped back seven yards behind the line of scrimmage. He bent over just as Chip had seen him do hundreds of times when they'd practiced in the backyard at home. Speed could do it; Speed had to do it!

Chip sat down abruptly. He felt tired and weak. He clasped the hard cast with both hands and closed his eyes. Any second now, there would be a roar of victory or a groan of defeat from the home stands.

There was a sharp thump, and even before the thunder of triumph from the home fans reached his ears, Chip knew the kick was good. Speed had done it!

The stadium erupted in pandemonium! Chip didn't have to look at the scoreboard. The Big Reds were *state champions!*

CHAPTER 20

Snake Dance

THE REFEREE'S arms shot swiftly over his head signifying a successful try for the extra point, but his action was slower than the crowd's leaving the stands and flooding the field.

Like a giant tidal wave, the delirious fans swept out onto the turf, engulfing the subs, the coaches, the teams on the field, and the officials. The players on the sidelines were carried along whether they wanted to go or not. Chip alone escaped. He had not moved from his hunched-over position. He sat still, fiercely holding onto the wooden bench. After the first rush passed, he looked up to see cheerleaders near the goal posts at both ends of the field as the crowd gathered. There might never be another day like this in Valley Falls. At one end, Dink Davis unfurled a "State Champs" banner and looped it over the crossbar as another helper secured the ends.

TOUCHDOWN PASS

Another scene developed at the other end as several cheerleaders displayed a large white banner with the Valley Falls coaches' and players' names written in bright red paint. Cheers erupted under each goal.

Then, Dink Davis, clad in his red sweater and swinging a gigantic Valley Falls banner on a long flagstaff, lined up the band and started a snake dance. The line went around the field, picking up marchers here and there until everyone on the field was in the act.

One by one the players were hoisted on shoulders while their families, teachers, and friends cheered them wildly. Speed, bouncing along, was laughing happily and looking everywhere for Chip. Soapy Smith was hollering and repeating over and over that he'd be at the Sugar Bowl all evening to autograph programs.

Chet Stewart, Bill Thomas, and Pop Brown were finally located and, despite their weak protests, were elevated too. The crowd groaned in mock dismay as Bill Thomas's 220 pounds were hoisted in the air. Coach Rockwell resisted strenuously. He was looking for Chip and trying to fight his way back to the bench.

The band was playing the "Valley Falls Victory March," and everyone was singing and bellowing out the words. Chip was watching with a happy heart but was afraid to move for fear he might get caught in the crowd. Taps Browning finally got back to Chip and stood close to his friend protectively. They watched the euphoric crowd make the last turn on the track and dance out the gate. It would be a long time before the hundreds of cars parked in the Valley Falls parking lot would move. Most of the fans in that long parade seemed to forget they had come to the game in cars! They followed Dink Davis and the band straight for a downtown celebration.

SNAKE DANCE

Suddenly, a powerful arm wrapped around Chip's shoulders. "You did it!" It was Rockwell, smiling his widest smile, happier than Chip had ever seen him. "You did it, Chipper!" Rockwell repeated. "You called the strategy twice—the Statue of Liberty play and Speed's drop kick. What a finish!" Unexpectedly, he hugged Chip and spun him around.

"I'm proud of you, Chip! I've got to get to a phone. Got to hurry! But you just watch tomorrow's papers. There'll be a story there you'll want to save all your life! How the greatest grandstand quarterback in the history of football won the state championship for Valley Falls! Looks like Mrs. Rockwell will have to buy me that bigger hat after all!"

As Chip and Taps walked slowly out the big stadium gate, they could hear far ahead the symphony of horns, bells, songs, and cheers. The gathering dusk was settling now, and in Chip's mind reigned a great peace. Who would have dreamed the little squad that had started the season with neither experience, size, nor football savvy would end up champions of the state.

Chip glanced up at his tall, loyal friend. He was glad Taps's troubles were over; Taps was a real friend. Come to think of it, Chip Hilton was about the luckiest guy alive to have friends like Speed . . . and Biggie . . . and Soapy . . . and Red . . . and Jordan . . . and Ted . . . and Petey Jackson. Chip Hilton had more friends than about anyone else in the world. There were John Schroeder . . . the Rock . . . Doc Jones . . . J. P. Ohlsen . . . Pop . . . Chet Stewart . . . Abe Cohen . . . George Browning . . . Bill Thomas . . . even the South Side gang.

Chip Hilton had learned a lot this football season. Funny, most of it had little to do with playing the game.

He'd learned to start looking beyond himself and reach out a hand—

He suddenly grabbed Taps by the arm. "You report to the Hilton A.C. for basketball practice tomorrow after church. You're going to take my place at center, or I'll know the reason why!"

"But what about you, Chip?"

"Don't worry about me! I'll get along. I've got another year left. Besides, Doc Jones said I might even be OK for the last half of this season!"

■   ■   ■

Star center last year, CHIP HILTON faces the basketball season this year with all odds against him.

Be sure to read *Championship Ball,* the thrilling story of how Chip meets this challenge and helps build a winning team.

A Note to Readers

CLAIR BEE is regarded as one of the greatest basketball coaches of all time. His career winning percentage of 82.6 is number one all-time among major college coaches. Bee's coaching influence remains strong, with many of his innovations still in use today, nearly seventy years after he began coaching. But, Clair Bee's list of exploits goes beyond his amazing career winning percentage.

Despite his diminutive size and lack of natural ability, he excelled as a high school and collegiate athlete until a football injury ended his playing days. After coaching one year of high school sports, he became the football and basketball coach at Rider College. His three-year record at Rider was 55–7, with his 1929–30 team being the first collegiate team to score more than one thousand points in a season.

In 1931, he became the head basketball coach at Long Island University, a small New York school with virtually no athletic tradition or facilities. By the mid-1930s, LIU basketball teams achieved elite status and played before packed crowds at Madison Square Garden.

Bee's teams went undefeated in the 1935–36 and 1938–39 seasons, strung together a forty-three-game winning streak, and in one thirteen-year span had an incredible 222–3 home record.

His innovative and brilliant coaching produced new styles of offense and defense that impact the game today. He also was the architect of the three-second rule and later helped initiate the twenty-four-second rule which distinguished and saved the NBA.

At the conclusion of his coaching career, Bee became the athletic director at the New York Military Academy. He then initiated youth sports camp programs, including the now-legendary Kutsher's Sports Academy, and mentored many college and professional coaches, including Bob Knight.

Clair Bee was elected to six sports halls of fame and received numerous honors and awards. He died in 1983 at the age of eighty-seven.

CHIP HILTON is the sports-loving teenager born from Clair Bee's imagination. Clair Bee began writing the Chip Hilton book series in 1948. Over the next twenty years, more than two million copies of Chip Hilton books were sold. Each includes positive-themed tales involving human relationships, good sportsmanship, and positive influences. Through this larger-than-life fictional character, countless young people have been exposed to stories that have helped shape their lives.

John Humphrey
VisionQuest
Dallas, Texas